CLARITY

www.kimharringtonbooks.com
Twitter: Kim_Harrington

CLARITY

Kim Harrington

SCHOLASTIC

Scholastic Children's Books
An imprint of Scholastic Ltd
Euston House, 24 Eversholt Street
London, NW1 1DB, UK
Registered office: Westfield Road, Southam, Warwickshire, CV47 0RA

First published in the US by Scholastic Inc, 2011
This edition published in the UK by Scholastic Ltd, 2012

ISBN 978 1407 13085 9

A CIP catalogue record for this book
is available from the British Library.

Printed and bound by CPI Group (UK) Ltd, Croydon, CR0 4YY
Papers used by Scholastic Children's Books are made
from wood grown in sustainable forests.

1 3 5 7 9 10 8 6 4 2

www.scholastic.co.uk/zone
www.kimharringtonbooks.com

To Mom and Dad,

for always believing in me.

Even when I didn't.

ONE

"You don't want to kill me," I said.

"Of course I don't, Clare. But I have to."

If I hadn't already been bleeding, with the room tilting and swaying, I would have slapped myself. I hadn't seen this coming. I had let my personal feelings cloud my judgement. And now I was looking down the barrel of a gun.

I had never thought it would end like this, me on the hardwood floor in my house, propped up on my elbows, begging for my life. On my right was the crumpled body of a guy I hadn't fully realized the depths of my feelings for until I saw the bullet rip into him.

I tried to use reason again. To buy myself just one more minute of life. "This isn't you," I said, pleading. "You're not a murderer."

"A couple of weeks ago, I would've said the same thing.

But you should know more than anyone how people surprise you. People can do things you never imagined they would. You think you know someone and then. . .”

My would-be killer shrugged and cocked the gun.

Then the world went black.

TWO
NINE DAYS EARLIER

"She's a super freak! Super freak! She's super-freaky, yow!"

Billy Rawlinson and Frankie Creedon popped up on the other side of the convenience store aisle singing Rick James, their heads peeking over the cereal boxes like prairie dogs. I rolled my eyes, and they burst out laughing in that cackling, annoying way that two losers with low IQs do best. You'd think we were in elementary school by the way they teased me. But no, I was sixteen, and it was the summer before my junior year. Billy and Frankie had graduated from high school a month ago, but I still wasn't free of them. They'd been teasing me since kindergarten, and they hadn't broadened their repertoire much. I'd been serenaded by "Super Freak" lyrics over a dozen times.

I took the high road, ignored them, and took my selections up to the counter. Unfortunately for all of us, they followed me.

"What are you buying, Clare?" Billy asked. "Candles? Crystals?"

Actually just a bottle of Diet Coke and a package of powdered doughnuts. The breakfast of champions. I kept my back turned and continued the silent treatment as I pulled a tendollar bill out of my shorts pocket and handed it to the cashier.

"Hey," Frankie's nasal voice implored. "We're talking to you, freak."

He poked me in the shoulder blade.

And that was his mistake.

I'm willing to overlook a stupid comment here and there. But poking me? Nuh-uh. I lifted my elbow up and brought it back hard into his gut.

Frankie let out an *oomph* as he doubled over.

I twirled around with a sweet-as-pie smile. "Oh no. Did you catch my elbow in your stomach while I was putting my change in my pocket? Sorry, Frankie. You should learn not to stand so close to people."

Frankie was busy trying not to puke, but Billy narrowed his eyes at me and said, "You'll regret that."

I took my bag and left the store, head held high. This wasn't the first time I'd had trouble like this, and it wouldn't be the last.

I've had *666* scrawled across my locker at school. You'd

think my given name was "Freak" by how often it was used in the halls. Snickers, whispers, and pointing fingers had followed me into classrooms more times than I could count.

I'd done nothing to deserve this treatment. Contrary to popular belief, I was not a devil worshipper, nor a spawn of Satan.

But I *was* different.

And apparently different was bad.

In Eastport, a tourist town on Cape Cod, lives a family of freaks. My family. I'm a psychic. My brother's a medium. My mother's a telepath. Tourists love us. Townies scorn us.

My name is Clarity "Clare" Fern and my brother is Periwinkle "Perry" Fern. What were our parents thinking? Apparently where their next tab of acid was coming from. My mother's name is Starla, though Perry found her birth certificate one day and we discovered she was born "Mary". That find didn't go down too well with her, and since we valued our lives we declined to share that titbit with anyone else.

We live in a grand Victorian house in the busy section of town near the boardwalk. My parents bought it when they got married and left the "spiritualist community" they'd both grown up in. It's a lovely old house, with no permanent ghosts, and we use the ground floor for our family business: readings. Not the bookstore kind.

Perry was waiting for me in the convenience store car park, and as I slid into the passenger seat, I breathed a sigh of relief that his car was still idling. It was an eight-year-old black Civic with 120,000 miles on it. Perry wanted a new car, but Mom would never agree to that while this one worked fine. So he started it each morning hoping for the *click-click-click*, but the little metal box refused to die.

I checked the mirror to make sure the two stooges weren't following us in their truck as Perry turned on to the main drag.

"Any trouble in there?" Perry asked. "I saw Dumb and Dumber walk in."

"Nothing I couldn't handle," I said, and Perry smiled.

You'd never know we're brother and sister. I share my mother's red hair, freckles, and petite frame, while Perry has black hair and creamy skin and stands just over six feet tall. Though he does have the same sky blue eyes as Mom and me, plus a small scar in his right eyebrow for a dash of mystery. This combination is evidently a recipe for the loosening of morals in almost all girls.

Perry spends most of his time chasing girls and hooking up. Living in a tourist town is perfect for him. Every week a fresh crop of chicks rolls in, and one week later they roll out. He's eighteen and headed for college in the fall. I pity those poor women in Boston.

Mom let it slip once that he looks just like our father, though we wouldn't remember. Dad's been gone without a word for fifteen years. Getting Mom to say any more about him would require torture, so we leave it at that. Perry and I are convinced that good ol' Dad left us and Mom is still too in love with him to say anything bad, so she says nothing at all.

Perry flicked the indicator and turned on to a side road, deftly avoiding the bumper-to-bumper car park that is Route 28. Summer traffic is pretty heavy through Hyannis and Yarmouth, but not as bad when you get to Eastport, mainly because of Rigsdale Road. Named after a pilgrim (because if we love one thing on the Cape, it's our pilgrims), Rigsdale is a secondary road that runs parallel to Route 28 and has just as many shops, restaurants, and motels.

We took a right on to Elm and a quick left on to Rigsdale and had to immediately stop. Traffic.

I sighed and looked at my watch. Nine fifty-five a.m. We open at ten, and since it was Fourth of July weekend, we were booked for readings all morning and would be busy with drop-ins all afternoon. I shouldn't have asked Perry to drive me to the store for a doughnut fix. Mom would not be happy with me. For a supposed free-spirited hippie, she goes psychotic over tardiness.

Two minutes later, we hadn't moved an inch.

Perry groaned. "What's going on up there?"

I rolled down the window and stuck my head out like a dog. A hundred metres down the road there were no cars at all. What was going on? An accident? I pulled my head back in before the humidity suffocated me, and turned the AC up.

"No clue," I said.

Finally a police car backed up into the road ahead. It had pulled out of the King's Courtyard Motel, which housed neither a king nor a courtyard, but did have cheesy Tudor styling in the lobby and only charged $79 per night. The police car blocked the road to let an ambulance and three more police cars leave. Now I was really curious. I didn't know our town *had* four police cars.

An ambulance alone wouldn't have piqued my attention. Heart attacks and drug overdoses happen every summer. But this seemed a little more serious.

Excitement? In Eastport? Nay! But I had no time to snoop around Nancy Drew style. The cars were finally moving and we were officially late.

"Mom's going to kill me," I said, only half kidding.

"Yeah," Perry muttered absent-mindedly, staring out of the window as we passed the motel.

I'd expected him to crack some joke to make me feel better about my impending doom, but instead he turned up the radio. It worked just as well, though. The loud music drowned out my thoughts and before I knew it we were in the driveway. Our Victorian is painted a colour I like to call "haunted-house lavender". Surrounded by an antique cast-iron gate, the house has high, arched windows; gables; gingerbread porch trim; and one tower. The sign on the front gate says READINGS BY THE FERN FAMILY.

I dashed into the empty foyer, aka waiting room, and dropped my bag of breakfast on the floor. Mom must have started the reading without us. I opened the door to the living room, aka reading room, which is long and narrow with tall ceilings and decorative mouldings on the walls. The windows are covered with thick red velvet drapes. One large candle was centred on the table and smaller votives were lit on the mantle above the fireplace.

My mother immediately looked at me as if I had spat on the floor.

"Nice of you to join us," she said.

"Sorry we're late." Perry swooped in and flashed a bright smile.

I shook the hands of the fiftysomething couple sitting on the other side of our long mahogany table. The wife was tall and thin, and wore a yellow sundress and a big straw hat. Her husband wore the tourist tuxedo: khaki shorts and a flowered silk shirt.

Rather than sit next to my mother so she was flanked by her children (as she prefers), I sat next to Perry. Mom would have to get through him to get to me. He gave me a quick pat on the shoulder. That's what Perry is best at: calming people down and making them feel like everything's going to be all right.

Mom sighed and clasped her hands. "Due to the interruption, I'm going to need another minute to get into the meditation zone."

She didn't need a minute. And she didn't need the lights dimmed and the candles lit and the chamber music playing quietly and all the other crap. Her gift worked whenever she wanted it to, she just had to listen. But the customers expected the hoopla and wanted the hoopla, so hoopla they got.

My mother's gift is the most dependable of all of ours. She doesn't hear voices all the time, thankfully, since that would probably drive her insane. But she merely has to focus her energy on another person in close range and she can hear their thoughts. The limitation is that she only knows what they are thinking right at that moment. So if they wanted to hide something, it was pretty easy. Many times, if I had a problem at school I didn't want to talk about and I thought Mom might be butting into my thoughts, I instead reflected on gross things like a dirty ashtray filled with cigarettes or scenes from my favourite horror movies. She'd leave me alone after that.

Mom cleared her throat and opened her eyes. "Mr Bingham, you're a nonbeliever. You think we're frauds."

Mr Bingham nodded. "You're right, but that doesn't prove anything. I'm sure eighty per cent of the people who walk through that door think you're frauds. Especially the men who get dragged in here by their wives. Men tend to be more . . . rational."

Perry gave my knee the claw under the table, a warning telling me not to give this jerk the claw on his face.

Mom then turned to the wife. "Mrs Bingham, you're a believer, but you're worried about what we'll say. You're wondering what we'd do if we saw that you were going to die soon. You're wondering if we'd tell you."

Mrs Bingham gasped. "That's exactly what I was thinking!"

A groan came out of Mr Rational. "Good guess. Again, probably eighty per cent of the people who come in here wonder that."

I piped up, "Did you know that ninety-eight per cent of statistics are made up on the spot?"

Perry kicked me under the table.

Mom tossed me a look that could freeze fire. "You're right, Mr Bingham. That is the most common question we get. The truth is, we'd never tell you you're going to die because, frankly, we can't see the future."

"Bang! So you admit it!" He nearly jumped out of his chair in excitement. You'd think he just figured out how to split the atom.

"You misunderstand, Mr Bingham," Perry said in his soothing, deep voice. "We never claimed to see the future. Our readings aren't like that."

"Then what do you do?" Mrs Bingham asked.

"The three of us work in tandem on your reading," Mom explained. "I'm a telepath, meaning I can hear your thoughts. My daughter is a psychic and receives visions from touching objects you own. My son is a medium and if any spirits wish to speak to you, he can hear and sometimes see them. Our readings are for entertainment purposes."

Mr Bingham guffawed. "This ought to be good."

"May I have an object from each of you?" I asked the couple and put my hands, palms up, on the table.

My gift's proper name is retrocognitive psychometry. Bursts of energies and memories leave imprints on objects, and I am sometimes able to pick these imprints up and see, hear, or feel them in my mind. What sucks the most about my gift is its unpredictability. There are moments when I clutch an object, begging for anything, and nothing comes. And though I mostly need to concentrate hard, there are the rare times when I don't want a vision and end up slapped with one. I can't force the gift to work and I can't make it go away. It is what it is.

Mrs Bingham took one of her pearl earrings out and laid it in my left hand, while her husband put his mobile phone in my right. I closed my hands and eyes, and focused. Flashes came to me immediately, and I had to take some time to make sense of them and put them in order.

"You bought these earrings somewhere special. You were very excited about them." I paused. "The store was . . . in something else."

"The store was *in* something? What does that mean?" the husband asked.

"Give me a second." I focused harder, then it came to me. "A cruise ship. You bought these earrings in a store on a cruise ship on your honeymoon. They mean a lot to you."

Mrs Bingham smiled. "You're right." Then she cast a look at her husband. "You didn't even remember that."

He shrugged. "What about me? Let me guess, you think I called someone with that phone."

I tried not to let him rattle me and focused my energy on the phone. I saw something immediately and my eyes snapped up at him. He drew back, looking slightly scared and rightly so. But I couldn't say anything. Mom always reminds us, bad news is bad for business. Focus on the positive.

"You were laid off and you'd been using this phone a lot to look for a new job," I said. "You recently landed a great new position and this vacation is to celebrate that."

Mrs Bingham clapped her hands. He gave a tiny nod. I gave them back their belongings.

"Now," Mom said, "if we could have a moment of silence for my son to gauge if any spirits are with us."

Perry lost the paranormal gift lottery, if you ask me. His ability is as inconsistent as mine, and depends on a lot of factors. He has to focus much harder than Mom or I do and is often left tired afterwards. And there has to be a spirit present, one who is connected to either the place Perry is in or a person he is with. Sometimes we have customers who don't have dead entourages with any messages to pass on, which leave the client disappointed. And when Perry's gift *does* work? Well, then he has to listen to a dead person talk.

Perry closed his eyes and took several deep breaths through his nose. His chest rose and fell, but other than that he was completely still. After a minute, he opened his eyes. "I have a Paula here with us."

Mrs Bingham squealed. "Mama? My mother is here?"

"Yes, she says she's your mom."

Mr Bingham rolled his eyes and crossed his arms over his barrel chest. "Prove it."

Perry cocked his head to the side. "Um, OK. She says she never liked you and she still doesn't."

His face reddened while his wife giggled. "That's right. Mama never liked you, honey, and you know it."

Perry continued, "She also says that she likes your hat and it reminds her of the one Grandma wore all the time."

Tears formed in Mrs Bingham's eyes. "That's why I bought it. When I saw it in the store, I remembered Grandma." Then her face lit up. "Is Grandma with you?"

Perry listened, then passed on the information. "She said sometimes, but not right now."

I heard the bell ring as the front door opened and closed, but instead of waiting in the foyer like the sign said to, the person barged up to the living room door and started banging.

"What the hell?" Mom stormed to the door, her long black skirt swirling. She ripped the door open.

"Milly?"

Milly stood in the doorway wearing one of her right-off-the-prairie dresses, her stockings sagging around her skinny ankles. Milly lives next door in a Victorian similar to ours, though not as morbidly decorated. The ground floor is an antiques shop that does pretty well in the summer months. Milly is one of those old ladies who survives on gossip rather than food. Despite her big mouth, we like her a lot, mostly because she accepts us for who we are and sends a lot of business our way.

"Thank goodness you're here. Have I got news for you." Milly pushed her way past Mom and into the room.

"We're in the middle of a reading, Milly," I said.

"This can't wait."

Mom said, "This better be a matter of life and death."

Milly grinned. "Oh, it is." Then she scratched her head. "Actually, not both. Just death."

I wasn't too surprised. Every morning, Milly read the paper's obituary section first.

"Well, go on then," Mr Bingham said. "You're taking up time we paid for. This better be good."

Milly widened her eyes. "There was a murder at King's Courtyard!"

My hand flew to my chest. I'd expected Milly to have gossip about some hundred-year-old person passing away in his sleep. Not a murder. So that explained the police and ambulance earlier. My heart beat wildly under my hand.

Perry sank back in his chair. The interruption had torn his medium connection to Mrs Bingham's mother no doubt. "How do you know?"

"Well, Ed Farmington had one of his garden gnomes stolen again so he went down to the police station to file a report. They wouldn't even talk to him! They told him to come back tomorrow because they were too busy right now. So, naturally he stuck around for a while to get some information."

"Eavesdrop," I said.

"Yeah, whatever." Milly paused for a moment to catch her breath, then continued. "A teenage girl was found murdered in her room at King's Courtyard. Shot!"

I felt my insides squeeze. Someone around my age. Killed. Here.

Perry nervously rubbed his palm back and forth over his chin. "Do they know who did it or why?"

"Not as far as I know. Rumour has it her wallet was right there on the nightstand with money still in it."

"Was she a local or a tourist?" Mom asked, worry creasing her forehead.

"A tourist," Milly said softly.

Perry and I shared a glance. The ramifications were now much bigger. Anxiety burned in my stomach.

"Oh, that's terrible," Mrs Bingham said.

Mr Bingham said, "Hey, you guys are supposedly psychic. Why didn't you see that coming and warn the girl?"

Mom sighed. "Again, we don't see the future."

"Yeah. You're a bunch of frauds."

I'd had it. My frustration boiled over. I turned to Mrs Bingham. "Do you know a Jane Sutherland?"

Confusion swept over her delicate features. "Yes, she used to be my husband's secretary before he was laid off. What about her?"

"He wasn't laid off. He was fired. The company has rules against sleeping with your secretary, even though your husband apparently has no qualms with the matter."

"Clarity!" Mom screamed.

Mom pulled on my arm while my brother tried to pull her away from me. Mrs Bingham ran out in tears with Mr Bingham following and yelling about us being liars and frauds. Milly sneaked out on her tiptoes. Our next appointment – a young couple – walked in, gazed open-mouthed at the chaos before them, and walked out. It wasn't even eleven a.m. yet. I hadn't even had breakfast. But this is my life.

Welcome to the freak show.

THREE

Around the age when most mothers sit with their kids to talk about how babies are made, my mom sat my brother and me down and warned us about our impending freakdom.

"There's no guarantee you'll be blessed," she'd said, rubbing her hands together in excitement. "But considering your lineage, I figured it's time to tell you what to look for."

My mother and father were originally from a small town in the Berkshire Hills in western Massachusetts that calls itself a "spiritualist community". Everyone in town claims to have some sort of paranormal ability and the most gifted families are encouraged to interbreed to keep the genes strong. Some marriages are even arranged.

My mother and father came from "good stock" – meaning the freakage went back several generations. There was no way to predict how my twisted DNA would reveal itself. The only constant from our people seemed to be the fact that abilities emerged in puberty.

I'd always known about my mother's gift. I couldn't get away with anything, for one. When I was little, Mom would always know when I was lying. Perry, being two years older and wiser, filled me in on some of his Mom-blocking tricks before I could get myself into too much trouble. So when Mom told Perry and me that we might have special abilities, too, it wasn't anything kooky to me. It was just a fact, like any other inherited trait.

Mom had explained that our gifts were like any other talent. Some people are born with a great singing voice or athletic ability and they only need to practise and nurture that talent, and it would bloom. Same with us. After our gifts began to emerge, my mother helped us identify, harness, and utilize them, just as her mother did for her. We realized what Perry's gift was when, at age twelve, he simply told Mom that Grandma said hi. Grandma being dead was the first clue.

When I was eleven, during a parent-teacher conference, my teacher told Mom that I wasn't concentrating well lately and she feared I wasn't living up to my potential. Most mothers would be worried. Mine was ecstatic. She came home and questioned me, trying to get to the bottom of the problem. I admitted I'd been having trouble. I kept finding myself pulled into daydreams, most of which made no sense to me. I had no idea that this could be my ability beginning to emerge.

I experienced my first vision in front of my entire sixth-grade class. After Cody Rowe completely messed up an easy maths problem on the whiteboard, the teacher dismissed him and asked me to come up and give it a try. I hated being the centre of attention, but trudged to the front of the room as told. With trembling fingers, I erased Cody's wrong answer. I uncapped the marker and found myself slightly disoriented from the strong smell and the feeling of twenty stares on my back. I closed my eyes, hoping to calm my nerves, then realized I'd forgotten the maths problem I was supposed to solve. I tried hard to remember and then the answer came to me. I wrote it on the board, with my eyes still closed, then stepped back to look at my work.

First came the snickers, then full-on laughter when the teacher ordered mc back to my seat. I'd rewritten Cody's wrong answer. I was so confused. Maths had always come easily to me. Sitting in the safety of my desk, I knew what the right answer was, and didn't understand why I'd written something different. I didn't realize that the "answer" my mind retrieved wasn't my own, but the one

Cody had come up with minutes before while holding the same marker.

Once Mom explained my gift to me, she helped me to control it, and I learned to decipher the real and the now from the visions of the past.

Right now, though, standing in our foyer with the Binghams gone, I wished we were just a normal family, with normal family problems.

Mom was on a rampage. She was angry with me for blurting out Mr Bingham's secret and breaking our "no bad news" policy. I was too rattled by Milly's report of the murder to defend myself. I took my scolding from Mom until she turned to Perry.

"You came stumbling in here after midnight last night. I heard you," Mom said, pointing her finger at his chest.

"He's a man now," I said, standing up for him. "He's eighteen, and he's graduated. He can stay up past twelve on a summer night if he wants to."

"Not if he's so tired the next day he can barely concentrate on work. This may be a family business but it's still your job!" Mom was raving, arms flailing through the air.

Perry didn't seem tired to me. Mom probably only knew he was from picking up on his thoughts. But I didn't want to interrupt her tirade further by pointing this out.

"It's unprofessional," she yelled. "Both of you have been totally unprofessional."

Mom stormed into the kitchen, accidentally crushing the bag of food I'd left on the floor and was counting on for a late-breakfast-slash-early-lunch. Perry followed her, then came back a minute later, texting on his phone. When he was done, he took my elbow and led me to the front door.

"We reached the point of no return with Mom," he said, opening the door. "She needs some time."

"We can't just leave," I said. "What about the appointments?"

"You mean the appointment you just scared away? We have an hour free now, thanks to you."

I groaned and buried my face in my hands. Then I grudgingly followed Perry to his car and got into the passenger seat.

Perry pulled out and joined the line of traffic.

"Where are we going?" I asked.

"To meet Nate at Yummy's. I'm starving. Plus, it will give Mom some time to cool off. We'll eat, chat, and by the time we get back for the next appointment Mom will be chill."

I nodded, knowing he was right. We rode in silence past gift shops, a pirate-themed mini-golf course, rose-trellised cottages, and clapboard-sided Capes until we reached the restaurant.

Yummy's started out thirty years ago as a breakfast-only diner. After the addition of a large dining room, an outdoor patio, and a bar, it was now Eastport's most popular eating and drinking establishment. Tourists love the chowder. Townies love the bar. Kids love the hot-fudge sundaes. And teens love to use Yummy's as a hangout. It was our Peach Pit, except we didn't wear designer clothes and drive Ferraris. Eastport is far from 90210.

As soon as Perry and I entered, Nate waved to us from a booth, and we sauntered over. Yummy's décor is overwhelming. Lobster traps are suspended from the ceiling. Anchors are in corners. Giant fish are on the walls as well as framed bragging photos of deep-sea catches. And, of course, there are bright blue Yummy's T-shirts for sale. The tourists eat that stuff up.

Perry shoved Nate aside, and I sat on the opposite side of the table.

"How's it going, Clare?" Nate asked. His unusually bright green eyes twinkled when he smiled.

"It's going, Nate." I nodded towards the menu. "What looks good?"

He winked. "The waitress."

Perry laughed at him. "Dork."

As long as I can remember, Nate Garrick has been Perry's best friend. He lives down the street, and they have been through everything together: their *Star Wars* phase, their skateboarding phase, their discovery of girls. But Nate isn't quite the womanizer Perry is; he's more the academic type. Nate used to write for the school paper and had done such a good job this year that he'd scored an internship at the local paper for the summer. He was headed off to college in the fall, majoring in journalism.

I considered Nate as much my friend as he was Perry's. I'd been hanging out with the two of them even more since I'd broken up with my boyfriend. I didn't really have friends of my own, but Perry and Nate never made me feel like a third wheel.

I glanced at the menu, even though I pretty much had it memorized by this point. Yummy's speciality is fresh seafood, which doesn't appeal to me. Yes, I live on the Cape and don't eat seafood. It's a crime, I know. Thankfully they also serve breakfast all day so when the waitress came, I ordered a short stack of blueberry pancakes and hoped the boys wouldn't order anything too stinky. My silent chant of "no clams, no clams, no clams" must have worked because they both ordered burgers and fries.

"So what gives?" Nate asked Perry. "When I called you about an early lunch, you said you guys were booked."

Perry grinned. "Clare had one of her foot-in-mouth moments that freed us up for an hour."

"Well lucky me," Nate said.

I leaned back in the booth. "Glad my inability to hold my tongue could bring you boys together."

"Did you hear about the murder?" Nate asked.

I nodded. "Milly burst in during a reading and told us. Speaking of which, shouldn't you be out there doing whatever it is reporters do?"

"Gathering information to write a story?"

"Yeah."

"I'm doing it. You'll see."

The door opened and a man I'd never seen before came in. Tall and broad-shouldered with tan skin and black hair, he was handsome for an older man. Just as I thought that, his younger clone walked in behind him. The younger guy's walk oozed confidence and his body radiated heat. He wore low-slung jeans and a black T-shirt that clung just so to his muscular frame. As he walked past our booth, he glanced at me with his dark eyes and then cracked a small smile. I nearly melted right there in my seat.

"Speaking of yummy," I whispered.

"He's why I'm here," Nate said.

I raised an eyebrow. "I didn't know you swung that way, but you've got good taste, boy."

Nate rolled his eyes. "That's Eastport's new detective and his son."

I sneaked a glance over my shoulder and watched them settle into a booth in the corner.

"Supposedly he's some hotshot from New York City, but he's moved here full-time," Nate said. "His son will be a senior this year."

A new hottie joining my school. Nice. "What's his name?" I asked.

"The detective is Anthony Toscano. His son is Gabriel."

Gabriel Toscano. Damn. Even his name was sexy.

"What would a city hotshot want with a small-town gig?" Perry asked.

Nate shrugged. "I'll find that out when I talk to him."

"So that's why you're here," Perry said.

"Yep. Our new detective has established a routine already. Grilled cheese and fries for lunch every day at the same time at the same restaurant."

"So what are you waiting for?" I asked.

"I'll let him have his lunch first. No one wants to be bothered by a reporter when they're hungry."

Just then, the waitress brought our drinks. I was about to take a sip of my Coke when I saw something floating at the top that wasn't one of the ice cubes.

"I think someone spat in my soda."

"What? No way," Perry said.

Nate slid my glass over to him and peered in. "Oh, that's foul, man! Who would do that?"

Our waitress seemed nice enough. I didn't think I knew any of the cooks at Yummy's. And then it hit me. I turned around and looked at the other waitress, who was leaning against the bar. She waved, her hot pink plastic fingernails glinting in the sunlight. Tiffany Desposito. The Lex Luthor to my Superman. The Wicked Witch to my Dorothy. The Maleficent to my Sleeping Beauty. I'm not exaggerating.

Tiffany Desposito is the queenpin of the Trifecta of Mean: Tiffany, Brooke, and Kendra. All three are blonde, though only Brooke was born that way. They're your typical mean girls, and during the school year, I am their daily target practice. For years it was only your garden-variety ostracism, name-calling (mostly variations of "freak") and pranks. But this past year, for some reason, Tiffany amped up the torture and made it more personal. And now I was staring at her spit in my drink.

"That bitch," Perry said. "Do you want me to go over there?"

"No, I'll take care of this."

I marched over and slammed my glass on the mahogany bar.

Tiffany fake-smiled. "A psychic and a medium walk into a bar. The psychic says..."

"Screw you."

She frowned. "That's not how the joke goes, Clare."

"You know where you can shove your joke. Just get me a new drink and try not to include any of your STD-laced body fluid in it this time."

Tiffany dumped the soda out and began to repour.

"I'd like a whole new glass."

She narrowed her eyes at me, then grunted as she reached for a new glass. "So how's Justin?" she asked.

I wanted to use an upended stool to pole vault over the bar and gouge her eyes out. Instead I took a deep breath and talked myself through it.

Remain calm.

Don't sink to her level.

You are a classy girl.

She is a psychotic skankbag.

You are the better of the two. Act like it.

OK, now I was calm. "I don't know how Justin is and I don't care."

"Really?" she said. "I thought you cared about him a lot."

Maybe she's suicidal? That's why she keeps inviting me to kill her? I fumbled with the coaster in front of me to keep my hands busy, since all they wanted to do at that moment was wrap themselves around her neck.

Then, suddenly, a shadowy flash came to me. Tiffany, taking an order, arguing with a girl. Shockingly, not me. Another flash, of Detective Toscano walking into Yummy's minutes ago. Tiffany nervously kneading a coaster between her fingers. The coaster I held in my hands right now.

Tiffany was scared.

Why was she scared of the cop?

"Hey! Space shot! You want your Coke or not?"

I tried to ignore Tiffany's screeching and hold on to the vision, but it blurred and disappeared. I grabbed my new glass from her outstretched hand.

"I heard you got into an argument last night," I said.

Tiffany paled, which I had never thought possible since her skin was so fake-and-bake tan. She nervously twirled a lock of her bleached blonde hair around a finger. "Where did you hear that?"

"Doesn't matter where I heard it." I took a chance and added, "But it was pretty juicy gossip, considering who she was."

Tiffany's pale face turned to green and I involuntarily took a step back, half expecting an Exorcist-style stream of vomit to shoot out of her gaping mouth. Instead, she narrowed her eyes and leaned closer. "Get away from me," she growled.

And then it became clear. My flash of her argument. Her fear of the detective. She'd argued with the girl who was murdered last night. And she did not want Detective Toscano to find out about it.

I stepped away from the bar, giddy with my new knowledge. I had the upper hand on Tiffany Desposito. I could torture her with this. Drag it out. Hold it over her head for days, even weeks.

"It's too bad you're not with Justin any more," she said to my back. "He's a cutie. And *such* a good kisser."

And that was my limit.

I spun around and dumped my brand-new Coke over her head. She shrieked and flailed her hands as the liquid streamed over her face and down between her giant boobs. She peeled her sticky hair off her eyes and snarled, "I'll get you for this."

I merely smiled, then sauntered over to the two Toscanos, who had apparently been watching this whole display with entertained grins on their faces.

"You're the new detective?" I asked the elder Toscano.

He nodded. Either his mouth was too full with French fries or he was too scared of me to speak at the moment.

"Tiffany Desposito, the wet and sticky waitress over

there? She had a fight with the girl who was murdered. Last night, at this restaurant. You should question her right away. I wouldn't even give her a chance to go home and shower first. I think she's a flight risk."

I strolled back to my booth, sat down, and tore into my pancakes, happy as a kid on Christmas Day. Nate and Perry stared at me in silence for a few moments.

Then Perry said, "Maybe you should have let me go over."

Nate shook his head. "Nah. She did just fine."

FOUR

The best thing about summer was being out of school, mostly away from Tiffany's reign of terror and my daily dose of persecution. The worst thing was that I was shackled to the family business.

I should have been happy we were busy in the summers. Appointments meant money and we needed money. You know, to live and all. And it wasn't like I had big plans this summer. But I sometimes imagined what it would be like to be one of those girls with no responsibility. To have the freedom to spend the whole summer on the beach. Or to lock myself in my room for a day with music on and nothing to do. Simple things that normal girls enjoy.

After Perry and I got back from Yummy's, the rest of the day's readings went smoothly. And Mom, as Perry had predicted, had calmed down somewhat. She even let me sleep in the next day, which was unusual. But you shouldn't look a gift horse in the mouth and all that, so I slept till eleven. I showered and put on my standard summer uniform: denim shorts and a plain white T-shirt. I dressed conservatively, especially in contrast to my mother. I figured I attracted enough negative attention, being a psychic.

When I finally made it downstairs, I found Mom pacing furiously in the foyer.

"Mom, you're going to wear down the hardwood," Perry said, coming out of the kitchen with a teacup in his hands.

"What's up?" I asked, stretching.

Mom took the cup from Perry, then settled on to the couch and sipped at the tea. "Our next two appointments have already cancelled."

"Why?" I asked, settling down in my favourite overstuffed chair. I slid the morning paper on to my lap.

"The tourists are fleeing," Mom said, a quiver in her voice. "Word is out about the murder and they're all checking out and heading back home to safety. July is our busiest month. If there are no tourists in July, we can't pay the bills in winter."

Perry scooted next to her and rubbed her shoulder. "Don't wig out, Mom. Listen to me. This is what's going to happen." His voice was smooth, with a dash of authority mixed in. "A few will panic, yes. But most of the tourists will stay. And you know how these things are. Ninety-nine per cent chance it was a crazy family member or something like that. Not a random killing. Once that news comes out, people will realize they're safe. The rest of the summer will continue as normal. Worst-case scenario our business is down for two days. That's it."

"He's right, Mom," I said, watching Perry with appreciation. Psychic gifts were great and all, but sometimes I thought Perry's greatest gift was his ability to talk Mom down from the ledge.

She nodded and took a deep breath. "OK, that makes sense."

I didn't mind the cancellations. It would be a rare treat to hit the beach with a book for a few hours. I was fantasizing about how I'd spend the rest of my day when I opened the newspaper and my jaw practically hit the floor.

A full-page ad displayed images of just about every psychic cliché: tarot cards, a constellation, a crystal ball, a candle. And it read:

Madame Maslov,
internationally respected psychic,
has come to Eastport!

What does your future hold?
See Madame Maslov today
to learn about tomorrow.

118 Rigsdale Road, Eastport, MA
Call now to book your reading!

My stomach dropped. This was not good. Not good at all.

"Oh no." The words spilled out before I could stop them.

Mom, sensing something new to worry about, rushed over and squished next to me in the chair. I cringed, waiting for her inevitable overreaction. As I gripped my elbows, she gasped. Then she raised her hands in the air in a silent plea of "why me?" Finally, she stood and began fanning herself while hyperventilating.

"What is it?" Perry asked.

"Madame Maslov," I said, rolling my eyes. "A new psychic in town."

Mom pointed at the newspaper like it was a dirty, filthy thing. "A full-page ad! Full! Page!"

Perry took the paper from my hands and read it over. "One Eighteen Rigsdale? That's right down the street. Hey, that's where Andrea's Book Shoppe is."

"Was," I corrected.

That spot was prime real estate, right on the boardwalk. A couple of months ago, the lease price went up and Andrea couldn't afford it any more, so she retired. I remembered my mother feeling so bad for her.

"First, Andrea lost her location and now this con artist, Madame Maslov, snapped it right up," Mom said.

"Let's not jump to conclusions about whether she's legit or not," Perry said.

"She claims to see the future," I said, shaking my head.

This wasn't good for business. First of all, people would much rather hear about their futures than listen to what we do, which is tell them something they already know. Second, it isn't possible to see the future, so this Maslov person was definitely a scammer. And anytime someone is scammed by a psychic, they generalize from that point on that all psychics are fakes. Scammers bring us all down.

"Let's not panic," I said, trying to prevent a complete Mom breakdown. I widened my eyes at Perry and tilted my head towards Mom, telling him to work his magic.

He caught on quickly, laying a hand on Mom's shoulder. "Here's what we're going to do. I'm going to head over to Staples and have the copy centre make a bunch of colour flyers for us. Then I'll distribute them around town, ask some people to display them. We can't afford a huge ad like this, but we can do a five-dollar-off coupon on the flyer."

"Five dollars off?" Mom was teetering on the edge.

"It's only temporary," Perry continued. "We'll put a two-week expiration date on it. Just to boost business in the short-term. We haven't lost any clients to this Madame Maslov yet and we have to nip it in the bud before it starts."

Mom nodded slowly, clearly thinking Perry's idea over. The phone rang and Perry jumped up to get it.

"Readings by the Fern Family," he said. "No, we don't." He frowned. "Oh, are you sure?" He paused for a long moment. "OK then, goodbye."

He turned around slowly. "Our three o'clock has cancelled."

"Why?" I asked.

"Because we can't see the future and Madame Maslov can. They cancelled with us to schedule with her."

Mom threw her arms up into the air. "That's it! I'm going to see Phil."

"What can he do?" Perry asked.

"I don't know!" Mom yelled, grabbing her car keys off the hook on the wall and tearing out of the door.

Perry looked at me. "I've got to get those flyers made.

Will you go with her? The last thing we need is for Mom to go crazy and cause a scene at the town hall."

I agreed and caught up to Mom, sliding into the passenger side of her Prius a moment before she started backing out of the driveway.

Phil Tisdell is a longtime friend of my mother. He's worked many jobs in town over the years and is now town clerk. Phil has a little crush on my mom, and watching her put lipstick on in the rear-view mirror made me think she was planning on using this fact to her advantage.

"I don't understand why you felt it necessary to come with me, Clare. I don't need a babysitter."

I was about to deny babysitting as my intention, then remembered Mom could read minds and had probably plucked that very word from my thoughts on the car ride over. I shrugged. "I'm just trying to help, Mom."

I followed her up the concrete steps to the heavy wooden door of the town hall. The building has to be over a hundred years old. On the outside, it has the look of a church that's been renovated into something else. All the town offices are housed inside. A large annex was built on to the east side of the building about ten years ago and that contains the police station.

We marched up a flight of stairs and into the office of

the town clerk. Phil was seated at a desk strewn with papers, both of his hands atop his bald head in frustration.

"I'm up to my eyeballs in dog licence problems here," he called out.

"OK, I can come back later," Mom said.

Recognizing her voice, his head snapped up. "Oh, Starla Fern! I didn't know it was . . . um, if I had known it was you that walked in . . . um . . . what can I help you with?" He ended his bumbling run-on with a wide smile.

Mom sashayed over to the desk, her long skirt billowing, her pink blouse perfectly fitted to her frame. I couldn't blame Phil for having a thing for her. She looked fantastic for forty. She kept in shape. Her fiery red hair had only a few strands of grey and fell over her shoulders in loose curls as she leaned over the desk.

In an unnaturally throaty voice she said, "I was hoping you could help me with some permit questions."

Figuring he'd be more likely to break whatever rules Mom wanted him to break without me there, I slowly backed out of the office. And right into someone.

"I'm so sorry," I exclaimed, turning around to find myself face to face with Gabriel Toscano. The hot son of the new detective. I realized after a few stunned moments that my hands were still planted on his chest from our collision. I brought them down to my sides.

"Sorry," I repeated, dumbly.

"You OK?" he asked. Long lashes framed his dark eyes. His black hair was dishevelled and he wore a T-shirt and jeans, same as yesterday. But as effortless as his style was, it made him look even more like an Abercrombie & Fitch model.

"Yeah, just clumsy," I finally replied. "What are you doing here?"

"I work here."

I blushed. "With your dad?"

"Yeah. I'm an explorer."

"Huh?" Was this some slang I wasn't up on?

"That's my title. It's part of a law enforcement training programme. I mostly run errands, grab coffee, and follow my dad around, but it'll look good on my college apps. I want to be a Criminal Justice major. Next summer, when I'm eighteen, I can be a seasonal officer."

"Cool." I pictured him in uniform. Let's just say the picture was ... nice. "What are you doing in the town offices rather than the police side of the building?" I asked, trying to sound somewhat professional.

"Oh." He waved his hand dismissively. "The mayor wanted to talk to my father and me about some stupid idea his son had."

I held back a pleased smile. The mayor's son was my

ex-boyfriend, Justin Spellman. And by taking a swipe at him, Gabriel had just landed himself on my good side.

"But I'm glad I ran into you," he added, grinning. "Both figuratively and literally."

"Really? Why?" I clasped my nervous hands behind my back.

"I wanted to thank you for that tip you gave my father in the restaurant yesterday."

I perked up. "About Tiffany Desposito? Did your father question her? Was she involved at all?"

"Unfortunately, she wasn't much help. She did argue with the victim about something petty, but her alibi is solid. She was working at the restaurant all night." He arched one eyebrow and gave a little half smile as he added, "But even though that didn't pan out, I will say that watching you dump that Coke on her has been the highlight of my week so far. From the little amount of time I spent with her, it seems like that was deserved."

He's gorgeous and has taken an immediate dislike to Tiffany. Thank you, universe, for delivering this boy to town.

He shifted his weight as if he was about to walk away, so I blurted out the first question that came to mind to make him stay. "Why would you want to leave New York City to come to Eastport?"

Then I immediately wanted to kick myself because it sounded like an insult. I added, "Not that I'm suggesting that your father downgraded or anything. I love Eastport. I grew up here. It's beautiful." *Oh, just shut up, Clare!*

He smiled. "Well, word definitely travels fast in a town like this."

Oh no, he thinks I've been asking around about him. Now he's going to think I'm a stalker.

"We haven't been in Eastport long, but..." He leaned closer, and I breathed in his scent – a mixture of soap, shampoo, and something intoxicatingly ... *boy*. "I like it already. A lot."

I began to wonder what it would be like to kiss him and had to force myself to stop and think of something else. I knew I was blushing and by the look on his face, he was enjoying my discomfort.

"See you around." He began to walk away, then stopped. "By the way, what's your name?"

"Clare."

"Clare," he repeated. "Cute."

My mouth was dry. My heart was fluttering. This was unexpected. After the break-up with my one and only boyfriend, I had pretty much resigned myself to a life of no dating until I got out of this town. But here was this smouldering specimen flirting with me. I was in uncharted territory.

Gabriel waved as he descended the stairs, and I caught a glimpse of the bottom of a tattoo peeking out from beneath the sleeve of his T-shirt. I tried to guess what it was. Barbed wire encircling his bicep? A gothic rose, perhaps?

Someone cleared their throat loudly, killing my fantasy moment. I spun around and saw Mom standing there grinning like a kid with a secret.

"Did you get anything you can use against Madame Maslov?" I asked.

"Unfortunately, no. She has all the required permits. The address is still zoned commercially. There's nothing Phil can do."

"Then what are you smiling about?" But as soon as the words left my mouth, I knew. "How long have you been standing there?" I hoped she wasn't listening in on my impure thoughts about Gabriel.

She covered her mouth to stifle a laugh.

"Mom, you have to stop listening! It's not polite."

She patted my arm. "Of course, dear. But only if you tell me what his tattoo says after you find out."

Mom's one errand on the way home turned into four stops looking for some new shampoo she'd read about on some hippie blog. All natural, not tested on animals, not bottled in any country she didn't like, squeezed from the extract of some leaf in a mountain somewhere. While held hostage in the car, I entertained myself by devising a plan to empty the bottle and refill it with cheap generic-brand shampoo and wait to see if she noticed a difference. Of course, as soon as Mom returned to the car, shopping bag in hand, she told me not to bother with my childish games.

It's really no fun having a telepathic mother.

By the time we returned to the house, it was late afternoon. We parked in the driveway and spied Perry on the porch swing, flirting with a girl wearing a bikini top, cut-off shorts, and Rollerblades. Perry was telling a story, his hands waving animatedly, and the girl doubled over laughing, slapping her knee. As we approached, he had turned to the serious segment of the tale. The girl said, "Oh, poor baby", with her lips turned down, while tracing his eyebrow scar with her finger. I wondered what the story was this time. Saving a Yorkie from a coyote? An old woman from a mugger, perhaps? The true story of his scar involved a rumble with our staircase. The staircase won.

"Where have you guys been?" Perry asked, as Mom and I climbed the porch steps.

"Searching the world for shampoo," I said. "Who's your friend?"

"My name's Jinnie!" she said in a bubbly voice, thrusting her chest out with delight. I guessed she was about sixteen and not a mathlete. "I'm on vacation here with my family and I was just skating past your house and fell on a crack in the sidewalk. Perry helped me with my boo-boo." She pointed to a scratch on her knee about as severe as a paper cut.

"That's my brother," I said. "Saving the world, one girl at a time."

Instead of a snappy retort, Perry grinned. "There's a client in the reading room."

"Why didn't you say so right away?" Mom asked.

"He only booked Clare." He grinned again, suspiciously.

"Oh," Mom said. "Well, I'm going to take a shower and try my new shampoo."

Mom went upstairs, and I stood outside the closed reading room doors for a moment. It wasn't all that unusual for only one of us to be booked. Sometimes repeat clients return with something specific in mind and only need me or Perry. I knocked softly, then opened the door with a wide smile, ready to greet my client. That smile quickly turned into a scowl, and I couldn't stop the words that leaped out of my mouth.

"Hey, douchebag."

FIVE

I had never expected to fall in love at sixteen. I figured I wouldn't even have my first kiss until I went to college with a clean slate, where no one knew me. I never bothered having crushes on the few cute guys at my school – because I knew I was untouchable.

Not because I was ugly. I figured I wasn't hideous by the way the boys looked at me when the girls weren't watching: their sideways glances in the hallways, the casual peeks over their shoulders while they pretended to adjust their backpacks. But none of them had the guts to stand up to mob mentality and date the freak.

Except Justin. He saw me with his own eyes, not through the judgement of others. He didn't care what the other kids thought or said. He didn't mind that I was different; in fact, he later told me it was what had attracted him to me in the first place.

One day last summer, he stopped by for a walk-in appointment, claiming he was curious about the whole "psychic" thing. But really, he'd been curious about me. He'd seen me in school and heard all the talk and instead of being freaked out, he'd thought it was cool. We started dating and by the end of the summer I was completely charmed by him. Places I'd been to a thousand times before – the beach, Yummy's, the movies – were much more fun with him. I'd never laughed so much in my life. Though I worried about what would happen when school started. But that was when I saw how brave he was. He stood up to anyone who taunted us and stayed by my side, even though it could have destroyed his own popularity.

But it seemed to have the opposite effect. The guys respected him, maybe for doing something they didn't have the courage to do. And the girls let up on me, for a little while. Don't get me wrong. I wasn't invited to parties or anything like that, but I wasn't tortured on a daily basis, either. It was the best time of my life.

But then everything changed.

Now Justin stood in our reading room, leaning up against the wall, arms crossed over his chest. He was tall, with a wiry athletic build. Usually, he was Mr Ultra-Casual, with sun-kissed blond hair that he kept out of his eyes by pushing his sunglasses up on his forehead. Today, that messy blond hair was clean-cut, and he'd traded his typical board shorts and loose T-shirt for a striped shirt and khakis. His father, the mayor of Eastport, was running for re-election. Since the campaign had started last month, Justin had become the mayor's sixteen-year-old sidekick. I'd heard he was spending the summer working for his dad down at the town hall, which would explain the nice clothes. What sucked for me was that the new style suited him. He looked even better, the jerk.

"I heard you and Tiffany got into a catfight over me at Yummy's," Justin announced with an overconfident grin that pissed me off.

I slammed the door behind me. "First off, I dumped a Coke over her head. That was it."

"Damn, a catfight sounded much hotter. I was picturing ripped shirts, exposed skin."

I rolled my eyes. "And second, it wasn't over you, egomaniac. You can date every girl in town as far as I'm concerned. I hate you. I pray every night that you'll fall victim to some strange and unusual castration accident." I pointed to the door. "So get the hell out."

His lips twitched, fighting a smile.

Ugh. I was going for "crazy ex filled with hate" not "isn't she cute when she's mad?"

“Feel better after getting all that out?” He walked around the table and pulled out a chair. “My father paid for the hour. So why don’t we both have a seat.”

I sighed and slumped into the chair. “Fine. What do you want?”

He sat opposite me and clasped his hands on the table. “Did you hear about the murder at King’s Courtyard?”

“Who hasn’t? It’s huge news. My mom is freaking out that all the tourists are going to leave.”

He nodded fervently, like I’d said the right thing. “Everyone in town is worried. Especially my father. He wants this case solved as quickly as possible. . .”

He let his words trail off like I was supposed to know where he was going with this.

“So?” I said.

“So, I’m here to ask for your help.”

I laughed out loud. After what he’d done, here was Justin asking me for help. He could go screw himself.

“Before you tell me to go screw myself,” he added, “just listen.”

I had to hand it to him. He knew me pretty well.

“The police haven’t released any details to the press yet, because they’re contacting the girl’s parents. But I’ll tell you what the police have told my father.”

At the mention of parents, I was reminded again that the murder victim was young. I felt a terrible weight in the pit of my stomach.

Justin took a deep breath. "Her name was Victoria Happel. She was eighteen, a tourist from Boston, here for a few days. She checked into the room alone. They're trying to figure out if she was meeting someone." He paused dramatically. "She was shot in the head in her room at the motel."

A lump lodged in my throat. She was only two years older than me. This was probably her first vacation without her parents. Maybe she headed down here with a boyfriend or some girlfriends, ready to have fun, swim, soak up the sun, have a blast before college started in the fall, with no idea that she'd never make it there. What had happened?

Justin was still talking, so I shook my head to clear my thoughts.

"Motel guests reported a loud bang at midnight, but it wasn't looked into. With all the action this weekend, there was a lot of loud music, fireworks, and drunks slamming doors. The next morning, the housekeeper went to the room and knocked. When no one answered, she figured it was a good time to clean the room, entered, and found Victoria. Dead."

My heart ached for this girl. "The police are working on it, right?" I asked.

"Of course. But they don't have much to go on."

I leaned back in the chair. It was strange having this serious, matter-of-fact conversation with Justin. It was the most I'd spoken to him since last spring, when that one vision had ruined everything.

One April night, Justin had come to pick me up for dinner. He'd said he had a surprise for me. When he walked through the door, he looked so gorgeous. I reached my hands up and pulled on the lapels of his leather jacket to bring him to me. But before our lips could touch, an image stopped me cold.

A vision of Tiffany Desposito playfully grabbing the very same jacket and working it off his shoulders. In the vision, Justin was obviously hammered, swaying in place with a lopsided grin. I saw Tiffany pull him into a sloppy, messy kiss. I saw her push him down on to a couch. I saw her climb on top of him.

I screamed.

I slapped Justin, who was bewildered by my sudden outburst. Then I pushed him backwards again and again, screaming, "How could you?"

I wanted to tear him apart, and he would have let me without even so much as raising a hand to defend himself.

But Perry came running downstairs when he heard me scream and pulled me off Justin and calmed me down. After a while, I was ready to ask some questions.

Justin was honest. He'd hooked up with Tiffany the night before. Some senior was having a house party and I hadn't wanted to go. Despite dating someone as well liked as Justin, I would never be one of the cool kids and never felt comfortable with that crowd. So I stayed home. Justin ended up drunk and with Tiffany. And they'd gone all the way.

I asked him if he'd slept with her because I had refused to. I wasn't ready yet. He insisted that wasn't the case and he didn't mind waiting for me.

He said he didn't know what came over him and had been so drunk he didn't even remember it happening. It was the first time he'd ever drank and he obviously didn't know his limit. The next morning, he'd woken on the couch in Tiffany's basement and she'd filled him in on the details. He said he'd never cheated before and it would never happen again. He regretted it, blah, blah, blah. But it had happened and I considered it unforgivable.

After we broke up, Justin followed me all over school, full of apologies and overtures, trying to win me back. After a month, he got the picture, but still tried now and then, mostly by phone or email. When I'd first seen him standing in the reading room, I'd assumed this was a last-ditch effort.

Now I realized this wasn't a social call. Mostly, I was relieved, but a tiny, stupid, irrational part of me was . . . disappointed. Despite the venom with which I spoke to him and the verbal daggers I hurled in my constant attempts to hurt him as much as he'd hurt me . . . I *didn't* want Justin to disappear from my life. I wanted to witness his guilt and his grovelling . . . because they were the evidence that what we had was real. We *had* loved each other. I wished my feelings for him were as clear-cut as I outwardly presented them. But they weren't.

"Will you help?" Justin asked, bringing me back to the present.

"I don't see how I can."

He grabbed my hand. I wanted to recoil, but didn't. "Your gift."

"You want to use me and my ability to catch you a killer?"

"You were born special, Clare. I've always appreciated that."

I knew he did. Justin had always believed in me, and my being different didn't scare him, it enthralled him.

Justin looked around the room. "Day to day, this is nice. Using your gift to entertain people. But, Clare, did you ever wonder if you were made for something more?"

I jerked my hand away. "I'm not going to let you use me to help your father get re-elected."

He blanched. "You really think that's my top priority here? I want the killer caught quickly to make Dad look good? This isn't about my father. It's about this town and the people in it."

I shrugged, regretting what I'd said. Despite his less than faithful past, I knew Justin would never put me in danger.

And he and his father loved this town. Though I would never admit it out loud, Justin was a good guy, with a good heart. He'd just made an unforgivable mistake.

"The police are doing all they can," he said. "But with your help, I think the case will be solved faster." He gently took my chin in his hand, forcing me to look into his eyes. "You could save lives, Clare."

I pulled away from his familiar touch. I had to admit, I was curious about the case. And feelings of obligation and duty swelled up in me as I thought about Victoria. If my gift could in any way help find a girl's killer, I should at least try. "OK. What do you need me to do?"

He sighed with relief. "Obviously you can't work in any formal way with the police. The new detective doesn't believe in any of this psychic stuff and didn't even want to work with you on the sidelines, but my father insisted. So they compromised. You're going to work with a summer part-timer."

My ears pricked up. "Who?"

"The new detective's son. His name's Gabriel Toscano."

I felt my spirits lifting. "When do I start?"

"Come by my father's office tomorrow morning at nine." Justin opened the door to leave, then stopped. "Just one thing. Be careful. I hear this Toscano kid's a bit on the tough side."

I smiled. "I'm a big girl."

SIX

Perry was lounging on the couch with a novel open on his chest. I snatched the book away and knocked him in the head with it.

"Ouch!"

"Be glad you're reading a paperback."

"What was that for?" he asked, sitting up.

"Why didn't you warn me that the client waiting for me was Justin?"

He smirked. "Maybe because you were too busy mocking my new friend?"

Mom came into the room, scrunching her damp curls with her hand. "Justin spoke to me on his way out. His father has offered to pay us for any appointments lost by your working with the police." She hesitated. "Are you sure you want to do this?"

I lifted my chin and straightened my shoulders. "Yes. It's

the right thing to do. And, to be honest, it feels good to use my gift for something more than a cheap tourist thrill. No offence."

Mom rubbed my arm. "Well, if you want to do this, it's all right with me. Justin assured me that you will be taken care of and not put in harm's way. He's such a nice boy."

"Nice?" I snapped. "He cheated on me!"

"One time," Perry said. "One mistake."

"I'm not getting into this again." I turned to leave. Mom blocked my way. She grabbed my hand and reached out to Perry with her other. "Come, fruit of my loins, we're going for a walk."

"Where?" Perry whined.

"Down the boardwalk. We'll grab something to eat for dinner."

I wagged a finger at her. "You're going to check her out, aren't you?"

"Whatever are you talking about?" Mom replied sweetly.

"Madame Maslov. You want to spy on her."

She threw her hands up into the air. "Fine. Guilty as charged. You coming or not?"

Perry and I exchanged a look.

"We wouldn't miss it for the world," he said, chuckling.

*

The first thing that hits the senses when you arrive at the boardwalk is that classic scent: a mixture of salt water, sunscreen, candyfloss, and Monty's pizza by the slice. The Eastport boardwalk stretches across three blocks and includes one arcade, two bars, and a handful of shops and restaurants. The only children's activity is the old carousel and the line for that is always long.

Tonight, as the sun lazily sank towards the ocean horizon, the boardwalk was bustling. Crowds were darting in and out of shops and eateries, and there were a few rollerbladers and cyclists, as well as two street performers. There wasn't usually this much action on Monday nights; the weekenders would be back home by now. But it was the week of Fourth of July, making this an extended weekend for most, and the boardwalk businesses were booming.

Including Madame Maslov's.

The storefront's large plate-glass window featured a pink neon sign advertising PSYCHIC READINGS. A line of people trailed out the door, waiting to get in. I took a peek through the window, but saw only a long red curtain. Madame Maslov's so-called readings probably took place behind that.

Perry sat on a bench, busy stuffing his face with blue candyfloss and watching the girls walk by. Mom paced back and forth in front of the shop. I had a horror movie Netflix double feature waiting for me at home, but now I felt my night slipping away.

"Well, we came, we saw, what else do you want?" I asked Mom, my hands in the air. "She's doing a great business. We can't compete with her location. Our coupon is making the rounds. That's all we can do at this point. Let's stop stalking and go home."

Mom wrung her hands and stood still. I hoped she was seeing it my way so we could walk back. Then Maslov's door opened and a familiar face looked out.

It was Stephen Clayworth, the only child of insanely rich Cecile and Dallas Clayworth. Whereas most guys his age were wearing T-shirts and flip-flops, Stephen went for labels rather than comfort. He was head-to-toe preppy, from his linen, button-down Ralph Lauren shirt to his leather sandals.

Stephen was not one of my biggest fans and I couldn't blame him. He'd graduated with Perry this year, but almost not, thanks to me. He'd started a fight with Perry over some girl. And despite Perry telling me not to get involved and my solemn oath to only use my power for good . . . I may or may not have tipped off a teacher that Stephen had cheated on a final. OK, I did do it. But he deserved it for messing with my brother. A dropped pencil had given me the vision and it took a sizable donation from Dallas Clayworth to keep Stephen's spot at the Ivy League school he was headed to in the fall.

The Clayworths own half of Eastport and can trace their heritage back to the pilgrims. Dallas Clayworth, the town's golden boy, is Eastport royalty and was now running for mayor against Harry Spellman. Dallas Clayworth's father had been mayor in his younger years and used it as a stepping-stone to the U.S. Congress. I assumed that was Dallas's plan too. And eventually Stephen's. Must be nice to have your life mapped out.

Despite how well Justin's dad was doing as mayor, some people in town felt he was undeserving of the office. He hadn't been born and raised in Eastport. He didn't come from money or a well-known family. He didn't have a law degree like Dallas. He'd been an elementary school teacher before he became mayor. But he was a great guy, loved the town and didn't want to use the position for higher aspirations. Mr Spellman had always been nice to me when Justin and I were dating.

It was funny. If Justin and I were still together, I'd probably be helping out, holding signs and handing out bumper stickers. Instead, I was staking out the new psychic in town and about to be accosted by the junior Clayworth.

"Checking out the competition?" Stephen sneered.

I crossed my arms and looked the other way, but he walked up to me and kept jabbering.

"Madame Maslov can tell the future, you know. That's something you can't do, Clare."

"No one can tell the future," Mom said, stepping closer to me. "We have free will and the future is constantly changing due to the decisions we make every moment. You should know that, Stephen."

He narrowed his eyes at my mother, then focused back on me. "Madame Maslov told me something about my future. Wanna hear it?"

"Sure, Stephen," I muttered, humouring him.

"She told me a little redhead was gonna bring me trouble. I told her you already had, but she said you weren't done with me yet. What do you think of that?"

I shrugged and put my hands in my pockets. "I think it's a load of bull."

"You know what I think is a load of bull?" he asked, raising his voice. "That Mayor Harry Spellman is letting this town fall apart."

Oh no, here we go. A pompous rant. Perry rolled his eyes, and I sighed loudly. I could be home watching zombies in high-def.

People walking by slowed their pace and some stopped

completely as Stephen's hands flailed in the air and his monologue went on.

He bent over to pick up a chocolate bar. "Like this litter on the boardwalk," he said. "And most shocking of all, a tourist getting killed! Tourists have never been killed before in this town." He poked my shoulder as he asked, "What is your beloved Mayor Spellman going to do about this disgrace?"

That snapped Perry out of his disinterest. He bolted over to us and shoved Stephen aside.

"Hey!" Stephen bellowed. "Don't push me!"

"Don't touch my sister," Perry countered.

Mom stood frozen with her fist covering her mouth.

Just as I thought they'd go to blows, a finely manicured hand appeared on Stephen's arm. He looked over his shoulder and immediately calmed and stepped back. Cecile Clayworth had that effect on people.

Her silky black hair hung evenly to just above the shoulder, where a handbag worth about the same as my brother's car hung. Stephen's mother hadn't been born an upper-crust WASP. Rumour had it her childhood was a rough one, spent in foster care and bouncing around. But she had big dreams and high hopes and the looks to match. Landing a man like Dallas Clayworth was a life-changing prospect and she'd easily moulded herself into a snob.

"I apologize for my son's behaviour," Cecile said, her voice smooth.

If there was anything Cecile Clayworth hated, it was a scene, and she avoided them at all costs. Anytime Stephen got into trouble, Cecile dealt with it by pretending it had never happened.

She took off her oversized Hollywood sunglasses and peered at the small crowd that had formed in response to Stephen's outburst. Her eyes said "move on". And they did.

She whispered something in Stephen's ear, and he immediately slunk over to the nearest bench and sat down.

She turned back to us and spoke softly. "You'll have to excuse my son. I think the election has put all of us under stress lately." She smiled delicately.

Then, as quickly as she had materialized, she was gone. What could have been a knock-down, drag-out fight (my money was on Perry, by the way) ended as quickly as it had escalated. Cecile came off as classy and mildly apologetic and before we knew it she'd steered Stephen away like a naughty little boy who had to go home.

"Let's head back," Perry said, putting one arm around me and one around Mom.

"You two go on," I said. I wasn't in the mood for a

movie at home any more. "I'm going for a walk on the beach, to clear my head. I've got to meet with Justin and Gabriel first thing in the morning and start working on finding Victoria Happel's killer."

Perry's arm fell from my shoulder.

"What?" I asked. "You know Justin asked me to work with the police on this case."

He only nodded.

What was his problem? Then, it hit me. Always the overprotective brother.

I reached up and patted him on the head. "I'm not going to be in any danger, Perry. Stop your worrying."

With that, I turned on my heel and followed the sound of the pounding surf.

I've always loved the ocean, the smell of salt in the air, the sand under my feet, the wind in my hair. Justin and I had spent many days at the beach. He'd given me my first-ever kiss over by the jetty. I had realized I was in love with him while we held hands under the boardwalk. Even in winter, we'd strolled across the sand, laughing as the wind whipped our hair into our faces.

I could have stayed with Justin. He wanted to stay together, swore he would never cheat again. Things would have been easier on me if I'd stayed. But my pride wouldn't let me. I broke up with him and returned to untouchable status.

I didn't go to the beach for a month.

I was glad to return now. The first time was bad and I'd shed a few tears, but now the beach was mine again and I could ignore the memories of Justin and focus on the beauty of the ocean.

I sank down on to the sand and closed my eyes. I was so focused on the rhythmic push and pull of the tide that I didn't hear footsteps behind me. I didn't realize anyone stood over me, until two hands squeezed my shoulders.

SEVEN

I bolted upright.

Perry backed up, hands in the air. "I figured you heard me coming."

I put a hand over my heart. "No, I didn't. You scared me."

"Sorry." He sat on the sand facing me. He looked strange, his eyes dull, his face slack, as if he were in shock.

"What are you doing out here? I thought you were going home."

He turned away and looked at the sea. The light of the half-moon shimmered on thc ocean, giving the small waves a metallic look. "Kind of calm tonight, huh? Not that choppy."

Nice dodge. I paused and waited for him to answer the question. When he didn't, I said, "You're acting weird. What is it?"

He turned back to me. "I was with a Vicki Saturday night."

I rocked back in surprise. "What? Who's Vicki?"

"I was with a girl Saturday night. She was eighteen. I never got her last name, but her first name was Vicki. Short for Victoria, I guess."

I swallowed hard. "A tourist?"

"Yeah. She took me back to her motel room."

"Don't tell me." I put my hand up in front of my face. If he didn't say it, then it wouldn't be true. If he didn't say the words, then maybe this wasn't happening.

"King's Courtyard."

My stomach twisted. "Who was she here with?" I asked, still hoping for this to be a joke or a coincidence.

His face shut down and his voice was flat. "No one. I met her at Yummy's. She was all pissed off. Something about her best friend betraying her and what she came to the Cape for wasn't working out and life never worked out for her and all that stuff. I tried to cheer her up, we got talking and then, you know."

"Perry." I shook my head.

He pulled his legs up and rested his chin on his knees. In that one motion, he stopped looking like my confident older brother and instead morphed into a worried child. "What are the chances that more than one Vicki was staying alone at the King's Courtyard Saturday night?" he asked in a small voice.

"Not good," I said. I chewed on my lip. I hated to even ask, but had to. "Do you know who did this?"

He shook his head and stared at the sand. "She was alive and content when I left. She wanted me to spend the night, but I wanted to get back home before Mom realized I was out so late. I left her there." He paused and added, with a catch in his voice, "And now she's dead."

I knew Perry was a player, but we usually steered clear of conversations regarding his escapades. I didn't need to know the details of his overactive love life. In this case, though, I had to ask. I braced myself for the question. "Did you have sex with her?"

He broke eye contact and mumbled under his breath, "Yeah."

My nostrils flared as a jumble of emotions rumbled inside me. I was angry at Perry for his reckless behaviour. Worried about the consequences for him. Freaked out about Mom finding out and having a breakdown. And furious at Perry's whorish ways for causing it all. I yelled, "You didn't even know her!"

"She wanted to!" He stood quickly, kicking up a small sandstorm. "What was I supposed to say? No? Clare, I'm an eighteen-year-old guy. When an opportunity like this comes around, I take it."

"Just shut up, Perry. I can't even stand to think about this."

I put my face in my hands. He sat back down and we both stewed in silence for a few minutes. Slowly, my anger receded. He was right. What single guy would turn that offer down? Yeah, the situation sucked, but it could be worse. He could have stayed and ended up shot, too. I couldn't even let my mind go there. I focused instead on the problem at hand. I had to protect my brother.

"Did anyone see you leave the restaurant with her?"

He shrugged. "I don't know. The place was mobbed. The Saturday night of the busiest week of the year; everyone was there."

"Who's everyone?"

Perry's eyes lifted up to the black sky as if the stars had the answers. "I don't remember."

"This isn't good, Perry." I paused, my mind turning with possibilities. "Keep this info to yourself for now."

"You have to tell the police, Clare. You're working with them now."

"I don't have to do anything of the sort," I said, my voice steady. All the competing emotions cleared. I knew what had to be done.

"I was with her the night she was killed," Perry said. "That makes me a top suspect. Hiding that information would make you an accessory or whatever. I don't want to get you in trouble for keeping this from the police or from Justin."

I stood up and dusted myself off. "Screw the police and screw Justin. Family first. Keep your trap shut."

I marched home with Perry following at a distance, head low, like a shamed dog. With each pounding footstep, my thoughts raced. Perry had done something stupid, sure, but I wasn't going to go to the cops and offer him up like a sacrifice. They'd waste their time focusing on him rather than the real killer.

Perry had nothing to do with this. Of course he didn't, I repeated silently. I glanced over my shoulder at Perry slinking in the darkness.

He couldn't have.

The phone rang at some ungodly hour the next morning and I picked it up, my voice thick with sleep. "Hello?"

"Clare, this is Harry Spellman."

I sat straight up in bed. Had I missed the meeting? I'd been up half the night worrying. I squinted at my digital clock. No, it was only eight. "Good morning, Mr Spellman."

"I wanted to thank you for coming to my office today to meet with Justin and Gabriel Toscano. I also wanted to apologize because I won't be at the meeting."

"No problem. You must be very busy."

"It's not that, Clare. I won't be involved in this part of the investigation at all. Justin will be acting on my behalf. Detective Toscano's son, Gabriel, will be acting on *his* behalf. The three of you will need to work together on this."

Mr Spellman was a nice man. While Justin and I had dated, his parents never seemed to mind my ... idiosyncrasies. In fact, they believed in them. I wondered if that had changed. "You don't believe in me?" I asked.

"Of course I do. I always have." He paused for a moment, then sighed. "I'll be honest with you, Clare. This is the first murder we've had in Eastport in many years. The townspeople are in a panic. They want to know the police are on the job – not teenagers, not our resident psychic. You know I respect and admire you and your family, but if I want to be re-elected, I need to keep myself out of any ... questionable predicaments."

I sighed, too. It made perfect sense. "I understand."

"The same goes for Detective Toscano. He's busy running the formal investigation and he doesn't really buy into this. In fact, he's only allowing his son to work with you as a favour to me."

"OK."

"I apologize again. But I trust that you will work well with Justin and Gabriel. I really think you're going to help us with this, Clare. And I appreciate it."

I arrived at the mayor's office on time. As promised, Mr Spellman was nowhere to be seen. Only Justin and Gabriel were there, standing in front of the mayor's desk. On the desk sat a plastic bag that my eyes went to immediately. Then I looked at Justin and Gabriel. Seeing the two of them standing next to each other was a jolt stronger than my morning Diet Coke. Those were two handsome guys. Unfortunately one was a jerk. I nodded at both of them. "Justin. Gabriel. Good morning."

Confusion fell over Gabriel's face. "Clare? What are you doing here?"

Now it was Justin's turn to look bewildered. "You two know each other?"

"Wait, wait," Gabriel said, putting his hand to his forehead. "Clarity Fern. Clare? Clare is Clarity Fern?"

I kept my smile on even though inside it was faltering. "Yes, we're one and the same. Why?"

"You're the nutjob?" Gabriel asked.

I felt like I'd been punched in the chest. All the air went out of me. They'd got to him. He hadn't even entered the school halls yet, but the kids had got to him. Told him I was a freak.

My heart sank. We'd hit it off so well. He was the first guy I'd thought of "in that way" since Justin. I had been instantly attracted to him, and he'd actually flirted back. I'd got my hopes up and now it was all over.

He was just like the others.

My mind reeled. I searched for a snarky retort. Grappled for an insult to thrash out at him, my instinctive self-preservation I'd practised so much in school. But nothing came.

Justin put a warning hand on Gabriel's shoulder. "Watch yourself, new guy."

"Justin, could I speak to you alone for a moment?" My voice sounded young and vulnerable and I hated it.

"I'll be outside." Gabriel stormed out. I heard him mutter something about "ridiculous" before he slammed the door.

I turned to Justin. "What the hell?"

He held his hands up in a shrug. "I told you he's a tough guy."

"Yeah, but what's with the name calling?"

Justin sat down and rested his elbows on the desk. "Apparently, he has a big beef with psychics."

"Lovely." So this had nothing to do with the other kids in town and my reputation. Perhaps even worse, this was something already inside Gabriel. That "stupid idea" of Justin's that Gabriel had spoken of yesterday was actually me.

"He agreed to work with you, but only because my father is forcing his hand."

I rolled my eyes. "As if I didn't hate you enough before."

"Come on, Clare. It's not like you're doing this as a favour to me. It's the right thing to do."

That was true. And now I had a more urgent motivation to get the case solved quickly: I had to protect my brother. "Fine," I said.

"Great. Let's get started." Justin opened the bag on the desk and pulled out a wallet, a tube of lipstick, and a mobile phone. "These were hers. You want to give it a try?"

I shrugged and picked up the lipstick first. Closed my eyes. Nothing.

I tried the wallet next. Again, nothing. I was glad Gabriel had left the room. So far I was proving to be completely useless.

Then I took the phone.

Instantly, I was sucked in. I saw only swirls and haze, nothing concrete, but the emotions were strong. I was crying. No, Victoria was crying . . . in anger. I squeezed the mobile tighter, focused harder.

You don't own him.

Her voice was loud, insistent. A muffled response was out there in the distance, but I couldn't decipher it.

Well, he obviously doesn't want you any more, Victoria continued. *He wants me.*

Static crackled. I tried to hold on as long as I could.

We'll see about that.

Victoria's words trailed off and I opened my eyes.

"What was that?" Justin asked, wide-eyed.

"I got something. I'm not sure if it's relevant, but it might be." I repeated what I'd heard. I wondered for a moment if Victoria could have been talking about my brother. No, they'd just met that night at Yummy's, right? That's what he'd said.

Justin nodded as I returned the phone to the desk. I felt a small swell of pride. I'd just got our first lead. Maybe I would be useful after all.

I looked over my shoulder at the door and sighed. "Time to deal with Mr Tough Guy, huh?"

"Good luck," Justin said dryly.

I left the office and found Gabriel pacing the hallway. I

tried not to notice how good he looked in his cargo shorts and dark blue tee. I focused on the fact that he'd called me a nutjob.

I was invigorated by the vision. My confidence was back up and I was ready to get involved. Figuring the meeting got off on the wrong foot, I tried to make nice first. "I understand that you have worries about working with me," I began. "Maybe if I explained my ability, that would make you feel better?"

Gabriel wouldn't look me in the eye. "Doubt that."

OK, forget nice. My guard went up like a drawbridge. I hardened myself and faced him like I'd faced Tiffany, Billy, Frankie, or any of the others time and time again. With the only defence I had. Words. "Listen, I gather you have a problem working with a psychic. Believe me, I don't like working with a jackass any better."

His eyebrows rose and his mouth opened slightly.

I continued, "Mayor Spellman is forcing me to do this as much as he's forcing you. So how about this? I won't get in your way and you don't get in mine. We solve this thing quickly and then we never have to speak to each other again. Deal?"

There was a flash of respect in his eyes. He stared at me for a moment while twirling his keys around his finger. Finally, he spoke.

"I'm supposed to bring you to the motel room and let you do your thing there. Then I'll bring you home."

He started walking and waved me forward, but I followed at a distance. I needed to take a minute to regain my composure. I shoved my trembling hands into my pockets and took a few deep breaths. Telling him off had salvaged my pride and possibly earned me some respect. But underneath my outer bravado, my chest was tight and a slight ache filled me.

Yeah, I was Clare Fern, tough psychic chick, member of the freak family. But if they stripped all those labels off, people might be shocked to find a normal girl beneath. Who doesn't want to spend her days on the defensive. Who wants what everyone else wants.

To be loved.

EIGHT

King's Courtyard was a single building of connected rooms that arched in an L-shape around an outdoor pool. They advertised it as "water view", but when you looked out of your window all you mostly saw was your car staring back at you. There were two floors. Victoria Happel's room was 108, first floor, tucked into the corner of the L, furthest from the office.

Yellow police tape stretched across the motel room door. I stood beside it, waiting for Mr Uptight to finish up in the office.

Only yesterday, he'd been all interested in me – flirting and flashing his perfect smile. And now Gabriel acted as if I disgusted him. I crossed my arms and tapped my foot.

He finally came along with a lanky hunched-over man, who I assumed was the motel manager from the room keys he had bunched up in his hands. Gabriel had told me on the way over that his father had called ahead, giving the heads-up that a "trainee" was coming to take a couple more photos.

"I'd really like to know when I can rent the room again," the manager said.

Gabriel took the key from him and began pulling a side of the yellow tape down. "It's still a crime scene. We'll let you know as soon as we can."

"But, see, there are people who would be willing to pay a premium to stay in this room. Murder groupies, you know."

"Sick," I said.

Gabriel tossed the guy a stern look, and the manager nodded and walked off.

Gabriel entered the motel room first. I followed closely behind, a strange feeling churning in my stomach. I felt like I was watching myself act in a movie or remembering a dream. Once again, I was reminded of how much of a freak show my life was. Normal teenage girls were at home, hanging out with friends, watching TV, flirting on the phone with their boyfriends. I was in a murder room.

Gabriel closed the door behind me. The blinds were drawn, casting most of the room in shadow. Gabriel flicked on the light switch and said, "This was the victim's room."

"Thanks, Captain Obvious."

I looked around. It was your typical cheap motel room. One king-sized bed ("We're one hundred per cent king-sized at the King's Courtyard!"), a nightstand with a reading lamp, telephone, and alarm clock, and a small TV on a dresser. The walls were dirty beige with one cheap painting of a sailboat hanging crookedly above the bed.

Gabriel sighed. "So what is it that you do?"

"Ever heard of retrocognitive psychometry?"

"Nope."

"It's the ability to perceive or see events that have taken place in the past. I have that. I touch an object, focus my concentration, and sometimes I'm able to see visions of things that have occurred when someone else touched the same object."

"Sometimes."

"Yes. Just because it doesn't work every time doesn't mean it's not real."

"I didn't say it's not real."

"I don't have to be psychic to know how you feel right now. I just have to not be an idiot."

I saw him almost smile, then remember he was supposed to hate me, and his face returned to a serious frown. "Point taken. I'll sit here in the corner and watch silently." He slumped into a chair.

"Fine. Is it OK for me to touch everything?"

"Yeah."

I went to the bathroom first and worked my way through there, letting my fingers graze, holding the shower curtain, the hot and cold handles on the sink. Nothing interesting came. Just grainy pictures of people performing their mundane tasks. I moved out into the main room and sat on the end of the bed, letting my hands rest on the bedspread. Immediately, it was as if I'd tuned into a porn channel with bad reception. Flashes of all kinds of sex came to me, but mostly indistinct. Red heat prickled up my neck and flushed my cheeks. I stood quickly, thankful that Gabriel didn't notice how embarrassed I suddenly felt.

When dealing with items that many people have touched, the visions can compete with each other and mush together into an indeterminate mess. I was hoping to pick up something of Victoria since she was the most recent inhabitant of the room. But it was obvious from what I'd just seen that the motel mustn't wash their bedspreads often. I needed to find somewhere that her touch lingered.

I looked around for the remote and found it on top of the television. I held it in my hands, closed my eyes, and concentrated. I saw nothing, but felt overwhelming frustration.

"Anything from the remote?" Gabriel asked. So much for him being quiet.

"Not a thing."

"That's good, considering she didn't use it. The TV is broken. She complained at the office the night she was killed."

That might explain the tremendous feeling of aggravation I felt while holding it. "It's too bad," I said.

"Why?"

"If the TV worked she might have stayed in and watched *SNL*. Not gone to Yummy's. Not ended up dead."

He shrugged. "We can't see the future."

"You've got that right."

He cocked his head. "Wait a minute, you claim you're a psychic but you don't believe people can see the future?"

"Correct." I moved to the dresser now, felt each knob on the drawers.

"Why not?"

I shrugged. "I've never met anyone who could. And, believe me, considering the population of freakazoids in the town my folks are from, if there were someone who could see the future, we'd have heard of them by now."

"What about that new Madame Maslov who came to town?"

"Scam artist," I said.

He laughed. "Pot, meet kettle."

"I'm not a scam artist!" I was so sick of having to defend myself to this loser. A gorgeous loser with a low, raspy voice and a great body, but still.

"Don't you think it's a little hypocritical that you get all mad at people who don't believe in your gift, yet you judge this Maslov woman the same way these people judge you?" Gabriel asked.

I had to admit – to myself – that he had a good point. But I didn't have to admit it to him. I put my hands on my hips. "Can you please shut up so I can concentrate here?"

He smirked, but complied.

I worked the room over for twenty more minutes with no concrete results. I needed a spot Victoria Happel had touched that wasn't recently touched by a hundred other people. But finding that spot could take all day.

"Ready to quit?" Gabriel asked with hope in his voice.

An idea occurred to me. "Do you have crime scene photos?"

"Yeah, right here in my back pocket."

I groaned. Wiseass. "Photos were taken, correct?"

"Yeah. What do you need to see?"

"I need to know the position her body was found in."

He stood and gazed at the bed. "I saw those photos. I remember. She was lying on the bed."

I paused. "I need to recreate it."

"Excuse me?"

I got on the bed. The sheets and pillows had been stripped, I assumed for the blood evidence. I lay atop the mattress and stared at the ceiling Victoria Happel had most likely stared at only three nights ago.

"Move me into the position she was found in. As exact as you can."

He shook his head. "This is sick."

"Just help me and then you'll be done with me for the day."

"I don't see how this is helpful at all. As a matter of fact, I'm starting to think you're completely wasting my time."

I had stopped listening to him. Something wasn't right here. I focused on a small, perfectly circular, dark spot on the white popcorn ceiling. I squinted my eyes. "What's that?" I asked, almost to myself.

"What?" Gabriel followed my eyes to the ceiling. "I don't see anything."

I clambered to a standing position on the bed and reached up on my tiptoes. Now that I was only inches away, I could see what it was clearly. I stuck my finger in it.

"There's a hole in the ceiling," I said.

Gabriel jumped up on the bed and examined the opening. "Definitely man-made, probably with a drill."

"It would give whoever had the room above a clear view of the bed," I said.

He nodded. "We'll have to find out who was staying in that room." He shook his head. "How did my dad miss this?"

"Did your father bother to lie in the bed and get the victim's perspective?"

"No."

"Then maybe I'm not just wasting your time," I said bitterly.

He blushed. "I apologize. This is a good lead. Thank you."

I lightly pushed him off the bed and returned to my previous horizontal position. "I'm not done yet. Will you move me into the position she was found in?"

He shrugged. "Sure."

He leaned down and placed his hands on my shoulders. Immediately, a rush of warmth coursed through me. I was glad he couldn't read minds because all I could think of was how devastatingly good-looking he was. And then of how twisted I was for thinking about that at a time like this, in a place like this. But I couldn't help it. I couldn't shut the thoughts off.

I looked up into his dark eyes, at his slightly parted lips, so close to mine.

Then he abruptly flipped me over like a pancake.

"Hey!" I snapped, my voice muffled by a faceful of bed.

"She was found on her stomach," he said.

"You could have done that a little gentler."

"Fine, no more hands. I'll just instruct you. Turn your head to the right."

I complied and took a deep breath.

"Put your left arm under your body."

It was uncomfortable. She wouldn't have lain like that for sleep. Maybe she was trying to push herself up and, after the shot, fell down on to her arm.

"Spread your legs apart more."

Thank God he'd stopped using his hands.

"Put your right hand on the nightstand."

"Near the phone?" I asked.

"Not that far. Not even completely on the top of the nightstand, more on the edge."

I reached my fingers out and delicately placed them on the wood. Then I lightly closed my eyes and focused. The room was suddenly cloaked in darkness. But Gabriel hadn't shut off the lights.

I was seeing the past.

Quiet darkness. Slow breathing. I'm tired. Satisfied, and

tired. The night didn't turn out so bad after all. A click of the doorknob turning. I smile slowly.

I lift my head up and say, "Back for more?"

I begin to push myself up on my elbows, then hear a loud pop! *Sudden, overwhelming pain fills me, then nothing.*

I abruptly opened my eyes. Between ragged breaths I said, "I saw it."

"Saw what?" Gabriel asked.

"The murder." I sat up, my hand on my heart, willing it to slow. "I saw it happen. She was lying on her stomach, almost asleep. She heard someone come in. She started to lift herself up and said, 'Back for more?' and then she was shot."

"Who did it? Who shot her?"

I tried to remember any details from the vision. "There was a shadow to the left."

"Yeah, that's where the killer was standing when he shot her." Gabriel prodded, "Go on."

My fingers pressed on my temples. "It was completely dark in the room. I could only make out a shadow. It's not clear."

Gabriel groaned in frustration. "That's very convenient, isn't it?"

I rolled off the bed and faced him. "Think I'm a fraud

if you want. What motive would I have to make this up?"

He counted off on his fingers. "Publicity for your family business. Money. Your own show on TV. Who knows?"

"What could I do to convince you I'm for real?"

He looked me dead in the eye. "Solve the case."

NINE

My sleep was plagued with nightmares. I kept replaying Victoria's death scene in my head over and over as I tossedand turned.

Back for more?

Back for more?

Back for more?

Here's what I knew. Victoria Happel was dead. She was shot in the head after having sex with my brother. After he left, someone came into the room. Victoria thought it was Perry. But it wasn't. It couldn't have been.

Because Perry is not a killer.

I repeated that silently like a mantra in the darkness of my bedroom while I willed myself to go back to sleep.

In my next dream, I was lost in the woods, unsure of which direction to go, and so tired that I eventually sank to the forest floor. I didn't move while insects nibbled at my skin. I didn't scream. I didn't wake up. Because, in my dream, I knew I was only dreaming and the little forest animals that bit and tore at me were only representations of the nagging doubts that were eating away at me.

Doubts about Perry.

I watch the news. I read articles. In most cases, the last one to be seen with the victim is the killer. But Perry was my brother. And had no reason to do this. Plus, he swore to me that when he left, Victoria was alive.

And Perry never lies? The chorus of insects laughed at my naivety.

I thought of all the stories he told girls, about his scar and other stuff. Lies, yes, but harmless ones, only meant to charm. *He lies to girls who don't matter to him. He doesn't lie to me*, I answered.

You just said it. Girls don't matter to Perry, the doubts chanted. *He finishes with one and moves on to the next. They're disposable. Their lives don't matter.*

Shut up! My voice echoed so loudly in the forest that I woke and bolted upright in bed.

I'd yelled the words out loud.

Mom burst in and the door slammed against the wall. "Are you OK?" She looked around the room, confused. "What are you still doing in bed?"

I squinted at the alarm clock. It was ten a.m.

"Sorry, Mom." I rubbed my eyes. "I'll get up now."

"Have you seen your brother today?"

"No, why?"

Mom sighed and clenched her fists. "He knows you're busy with the police department, and he promised me he'd work all day. This is going to be a busy day. The fireworks are tonight on the beach. We're going to have lots of foot traffic going by, lots of business. We have a drop-in waiting already, and Perry's flaked out on me."

I pushed my Perry-related nightmares out of my head. I couldn't think about that now.

I threw off the blanket and eased my legs over the side of the bed. "I can do the reading with you."

Mom's face lit up. "Really? You don't mind? I know you're busy."

"It's no problem. Gabriel hasn't called me yet." I stood and stretched. "Give me five minutes."

I didn't have time to shower, so I splashed some cold water on my face and pulled my hair up into a ponytail. I threw on a grey T-shirt and navy shorts and dabbed a bit of lipgloss on to my lips.

I rushed downstairs, pausing only when the morning paper caught my eye. It was folded on the coffee table bearing the headline, FEW LEADS IN TEEN'S DEATH. I picked it up and stared at a photo of Victoria Happel. Despite having seen her death in my mind's eye, I'd never seen her face. My visions are from the point of view of the original person.

Victoria didn't look like a typical eighteen-year-old. She was model-pretty, with long dark hair, a voluptuous body, and brown eyes that seemed older, more mature, with a come-hither look to them. There was a hint of a smile forming at the corner of her mouth and I was filled with sadness for her. She'd never smile again.

Mom coughed from the reading room. I dropped the newspaper and hurried in. The scene was set – dimmed lights, soft music, flickering candles. The client, a girl only a little older than me, sat up straight as I entered. She looked like she needed a shower and a full night's sleep. She may have even had a worse night than me.

"I couldn't find my son," Mom said, "but my daughter will join us."

The girl nodded slowly, her eyes vacant.

"What's your name?" Mom asked.

"Joni," she said, in barely a whisper. Her long brown hair hung limp like a curtain covering half her face. She picked at a ragged fingernail. The others were bitten down to the quick.

"How did you hear about us?" I asked.

"I saw your flyer downtown. I recently lost a friend." She chewed on her lip for a moment, seemingly deciding how much to tell us. "I'm here because I want to know if she hates me."

The phrase "lost a friend" raised goosebumps on my arms.

"You two had a fight," Mom said.

Joni's eyes snapped towards Mom. "How did you know that?" Then she reddened. "Oh, psychic, yeah. I'm sorry. I just . . . I guess I didn't expect this to be legit."

"Then why bother coming?" I asked.

She shrugged. "In the small chance that you were for real, I guess. And if not, then maybe it would help to talk."

I could understand that. "How my gift works is that I need an object to hold."

She nodded vigorously, pulled something out of her pocket, and handed it to me. I held it up to the candlelight. It was a necklace, with a charm swinging from the bottom. Half of a heart and a few letters that would say BEST FRIENDS when connected to the rest. My eyes went to Joni's collarbone and found the other half.

I palmed the charm and opened my mind to the feelings and vibrations coming from it. The most recent were sadness and anger.

"You betrayed your friend," I said, opening my eyes. "And now she's dead."

A solitary tear slipped down Joni's cheek. "It's my fault. Vicki's dead because of me."

Vicki.

Mom and I exchanged a look that said, "Yep, *that* Vicki." My pulse raced. This girl could have all the answers we were looking for.

"I don't see how it's your fault," I said to Joni.

The girl didn't meet my eye as she spoke in a rush. "She wouldn't even be down here if it wasn't for me. She ... fled or something. I think she came here to get away. To get away from me, from what I'd done." The words came out in gasps. "If everything hadn't happened ... if I had been a good friend ... she'd be alive now."

"Start at the beginning." I rubbed my thumb over the charm again and a name came to me. "Start with ... Joel."

Joni's eyes lit up with something like fear. "You got that from the necklace?"

I nodded slowly.

Joni settled down further in her seat. "Joel was Vicki's boyfriend. We all went to high school together. We graduated this year. But he ... cheated on her. With me."

Classic. What else are best friends for? At least the vision I'd had while holding Victoria's mobile phone made sense now. I remembered the angry words I had heard Victoria speak: *Well, he obviously doesn't want you any more. He wants me.*

"I felt guilty about it," Joni continued. "I told him I was going to tell her."

She stopped, and Mom filled in what she didn't want to say. "He got violent."

Joni nodded. "He pushed me up against the wall. Bruised my arm. He told me I'd say nothing. And the truth is, I never had any intention of telling Vicki what we did. I didn't want to hurt her or lose our friendship."

"Then why did you threaten to blab?" I asked. "To scare him. Maybe he'd tell her himself or maybe just dump her."
"You wanted her to know, but were too gutless to tell her yourself," I said.

Mom squeezed my knee under the table, and I knew I was getting close to the line. We never wanted to insult our clients, no matter how despicable they might have seemed.

"You're right," Joni said. "She's the best friend I ever had, and look what I did to her. She deserved better than both me and Joel." Joni's shoulders shook as her face fell into her hands.

"But you did gather the courage to tell her," Mom prodded.

Joni sniffed and lifted her face back to us. "I wanted Joel out of her life at that point. If he pushed me, who knows what he'd ever do to her if she broke up with him."

My thoughts were racing. Maybe Joel had seen Victoria with Perry that night and killed her in a jealous rage. I was suddenly filled with relief. Both that Perry hadn't done this, and that Joel hadn't killed my brother, too, instead of just Victoria.

The room stayed silent for a few moments. Then Joni continued, "I wanted them broken up. Vicki had already figured that Joel was cheating on her and the night before she left, they had a huge fight. She told him they were done. I should have just kept my mouth shut. But I figured, this has gone on long enough, let the whole truth come out. So I told her I was the one Joel was screwing around with."

"How did she take the news?" I asked.

"She went crazy." Joni fingered the charm on her neck. "That's when she gave me back the other half of the charm. Said we weren't friends any more. We'd never be again." Joni's shoulders slumped. "Vicki left town. I figured after the long weekend maybe she'd calm down a bit and we could talk again when she got back. Mend fences maybe. Now we'll never talk again."

"She really came here alone?" I asked.

"I guess." Joni shrugged. "Though that really doesn't seem like her."

"Did she know anyone down here?" Mom asked.

"Not that I know of, but..."

I leaned forward. "But what?"

"In the weeks before everything blew up, I felt like Vicki was keeping a secret from me. I was paranoid, so I assumed she was starting to put two and two together about Joel and me. But she really didn't know about that. So . . . maybe she was keeping a secret of her own."

"Did Joel know she was coming down here?" I asked.

"No, but it wasn't hard to find out. Her mom told me where she went."

"Might he have come down and..."

"Killed her?" Joni finished for me. "Probably. I don't know anyone else who would. She had no issues with anyone else. Just the worst luck in the world and poor judgement. Look at who she chose to be her boyfriend and her best friend." She stared down at the table. "Stupid girl."

"You need to talk to the police," I said. "To tell them what you know."

She pushed her seat back. "No. I don't want to get dragged into this."

I wondered if I could talk her into it, but one look at

Mom told me all I needed to know. Mom was reading her thoughts and the thoughts were all about flight.

Joni couldn't leave, though. She needed to tell the police about Joel. Before they found out about Perry and directed their attention towards him instead.

I was glad Gabriel and I had exchanged numbers for work. I slipped my hands under the table and texted him from my mobile.

TELL COPS 2 COME 2 MY HOUSE NOW!

My mother offered Joni a water, which she gulped in one minute. I kept her lingering a little longer with a more pleasant vision I'd plucked from the charm.

"I see you and Vicki, dressed the same, in white shirts and black bow ties. You're whispering and laughing."

"We're cater-waiters," Joni said, still using the present tense for her lost friend. "We work these fancy parties and stuff in the city. It pays pretty good, but we also have a fun time."

Joni seemed to enjoy hearing the memories, but was still antsy. She got up to go.

"Come back again if you want another reading, or even if you just need to talk," Mom said, walking her to the foyer.

Then the door opened and Anthony and Gabriel Toscano walked in. Gabriel's dark eyes were intense with concern and I realized my text had been kind of vague. He'd probably thought I needed help.

And had rushed over himself instead of just sending someone else.

I forced myself not to think about that, or how hot he looked at the moment, and focused on the issue at hand: Joni.

"Detective Toscano," I said to Gabriel's dad. "Thanks for coming."

Joni took a giant step back.

"Joni here," I said to Gabriel, "just finished her reading. She was Victoria Happel's best friend. She wanted me to call you over here so she could fill you in on what she knows. Particularly about Victoria's ex-boyfriend."

Joni glared at me, clearly furious that I'd deceived her. I felt a little guilty. But she'd betrayed her best friend. The least she could do was take a few minutes to offer important information to the police. Then Perry would be in the clear and this could all be over. Joni would be glad I made her do the right thing.

Detective Toscano took Joni gently by the arm. "We'll talk quickly at the station, then you can go on your way."

"Yeah, sure," she mumbled.

Gabriel turned to me before they left. "Can you meet

me for lunch at Yummy's in an hour? I want to go over some things."

"No problem," I replied, wondering what these "things" were and hoping they had nothing to do with Perry.

Mom closed the door after they left and sank down on to the couch with a sigh.

"I did the right thing by getting Gabriel and his dad over here, right?" I asked. "I mean, Joni wasn't going to offer up what she knew. She was going to disappear because she's too selfish to take the time."

"She *was* going to disappear," Mom said, nodding. "She most certainly doesn't want to get involved in the investigation. She doesn't want to talk to the police. Definitely doesn't want to tell them about Joel. But not because she's selfish."

"Then why?"

"Because she's scared."

TEN

The first thing I did as I walked into Yummy's was scan the place for evil waitresses, but thankfully Skanky McSkankbag wasn't working. I found Gabriel in what I knew was his usual booth. His eyes lit up at first when he saw me, then he did that forced frown thing again. I sat down across from him. "What did you want to go over with me?"

He frowned again, genuinely this time. "No 'hello'? No 'how was your day?'"

I'd figured he'd want to skip the small talk since he obviously couldn't stand me. I shrugged and picked up a menu.

After a few moments of silence, Gabriel cleared his throat. "Yesterday in the mayor's office, I noticed you're familiar with his son, Justin. Are you two close?"

"No." I certainly wasn't going to get into that story with Gabriel.

"Do you have a history?"

What was this? First he'd acted interested in me. Then he found out I was a psychic and treated me like a criminal. And now he was jealous of Justin. Consistent feelings much?

I lowered the menu. "Why wouldn't your father work with me on the case? Why did he make you work with me instead? And what's your beef with psychics anyway?"

He clenched his jaw. "It's personal."

"So is my history with Justin." I picked the menu back up.

We sat in silence until the waitress took our order and our face-hiding menus. I removed my mobile from my shorts pocket and texted Perry. Where was he? Not that I was mad for having to work; that reading had given us our biggest lead. But it was unlike Perry to run off on Mom without a word.

Especially considering what was going on around him.

The waitress brought our drinks and I took a long sip of my soda. "How did things go with Joni?" I asked after a moment. "Did she tell your father about Joel, the boyfriend?"

"Yeah, he's the main suspect now. As soon as he's found, he'll be brought in for questioning."

I had to point out the obvious. "You have my mother

and I to thank for getting her to talk. Joni was about to run. She wants no part of this."

He rubbed his chin. "I was thinking about that. You'd think a best friend, especially one with a guilty conscience, would want to help."

I stirred my drink with the straw, the ice cubes clinking against the glass. "My mother told me Joni's scared of Joel."

"Did she tell your mother that?"

Tell? Not the word I'd use, but if we were going to get through this lunch without fighting, I wasn't about to tell him my mother plucked Joni's fear of Joel from her thoughts. Thankfully, I was saved by the interruption of our food arriving. Gabriel took a bite of his sandwich while I poured the little plastic cup of dressing on to my salad and redirected the conversation.

"What else is going on with the case?"

He paused a moment while he finished chewing. "Turns out Yummy's has a security camera, fixed on the corner of the building, to watch activity in the car park."

I nearly choked on my lettuce. That tape would show Perry leaving with Victoria. "Really?"

"They propped it up there years ago when they had a problem with people unlawfully using their dumpster. But they never updated it. It's a dinosaur. They still use VHS tapes." He shook his head at the lack of technological sophistication. "The manager changes the tape every day and keeps a week's worth at a time. Of course they don't have the tape from that night. And since the office is unlocked and unprotected and a complete mess, they don't even know if it was stolen or misplaced."

"That's too bad," I said half-heartedly.

He nodded as he chewed through a bite. "But we did find out who was in the motel room above the victim. Ever heard of a guy named William Rawlinson?"

"Billy?" Why was I not surprised? I set down my fork. I hadn't thought of Billy Rawlinson since our run-in at the convenience store, but even that jerk's name was enough to make me lose my appetite.

Gabriel nodded. "I figured you'd know him. The motel manager said he's a townie and a bit of a troublemaker."

"Billy and his best friend are idiots. I'm shocked they managed to graduate last year. What else did the manager say about him?"

"He rented the room for the entire summer and recently started working as a maintenance guy for the motel."

"Glad to hear he's not mooching off his parents at least. I figured he'd live at home till he was forty."

"You don't sound like a fan."

I fiddled with my straw again. "Put it this way. I'm not

shocked that he drilled a hole in his floor so he could watch the goings-on on the bed below."

"You think that's why he made the peephole?"

"Yeah, he's a perv. Why else would he?" I paused. "Wait, you're thinking of him as a suspect?"

"You don't think he's capable of murdering someone?"

I thought for a moment. This was a guy I'd known since kindergarten. I hated his guts, but still. "I don't know. He's a bully, sure. But a murderer? I guess anything's possible."

Then it hit me that if the police had Billy, Billy may have seen Perry in the motel room that night . . . and blabbed to the cops. "What did he say about the hole when you brought him in? Was he in his room that night? Did he see anyone in there with the victim?" I asked, with a nervous edge to my voice.

Gabriel's dark eyes studied my face. "Is there something you're not telling me?"

"Of course not." I brought my hands down to my lap.

Gabriel stared at me for a moment longer. "The police would love to ask Billy those questions, but unfortunately no one can find him. The motel's manager hasn't seen him since Saturday morning, when he worked on a malfunctioning air-conditioning unit."

"And the murder happened Saturday night. So he hasn't been seen by anyone since then?"

"The police asked at the motel and at his parents' home. No one's seen him."

"Find a guy named Frankie Creedon and you'll find Billy. They share a brain. One can't survive without the other."

Gabriel reached into his pocket and pulled out a folded piece of paper. "What about this thing tonight?"

He slid it across the table, and I unfolded it. It was a flyer for the fireworks that night.

30th Annual Eastport Fireworks Spectacular
on Town Beach!
A night of musical entertainment,
games, food, fireworks, and celebration.

"Were you planning on going?" Gabriel asked.

"Most of the town goes every year."

"So there's a chance these two guys would be there?"

I shrugged. "Sure."

"Let's go then."

I hesitated. "Together?"

"You've got a problem with that?"

Was he warming up to me? Maybe he was changing his mind, going back to his first impression. Or maybe he just needed me there to identify Frankie.

Yeah, probably that, Clare. Check your ego.

I smiled. "No problem at all. Let's meet at my house. We can walk from there."

As Gabriel dug into his food, I discreetly checked my phone again. No reply from Perry. Where could he be? He never cut out on work, on the family's livelihood.

Another explanation whispered from the back of my mind. I shook my head. He wouldn't have run. No way.

Only the guilty run.

Five minutes till showtime and I was standing in my bra and panties. Three outfits were strewn across my bedroom. I'd dismissed the black Gap T-shirt and khaki shorts as too casual. Tossed the light sundress back on the bed – too frumpy. I'd torn off the tight minidress – too desperate. What the hell was I doing? Why was I trying on multiple outfits? Was I trying to impress a guy who thought I was a nutcase?

I sighed and picked up the sundress. I can't wear red, but pale pink actually works well with my hair. True, the dress was on the frumpy side, but it was comfortable. I was working tonight, not out to pick up guys. Especially not anyone in particular.

Thankfully, Gabriel was five minutes late and by the time he knocked on the door I'd just finished putting on lipstick and slipping my feet into sandals. I opened the door.

"I hope I didn't keep you wait. . ." His voice drifted off as he quite blatantly checked me out.

"What?" I asked, hand on my hip.

He flashed me a devilish grin. "The little pink dress. You look cute."

What I found frumpy, he found cute. Wonder what his response would have been to the tight number. My eyes gave him a discreet once-over. He wore jeans and a Yankees T-shirt. It wasn't exactly going to win over the locals, but I had to admit, he filled the shirt out ridiculously well. His short black hair was damp, like he'd just taken a shower. I felt my face begin to flush, so I turned away. "Come on in."

He stopped and surveyed the foyer. "I was only here for a minute when we came to get Joni. I didn't get a chance to check the place out." He paused. "It's not what I was expecting."

"What *were* you expecting? Voodoo dolls hung from the ceiling?"

He smirked. "Maybe just a little one of me."

"That's hidden under my bed."

He gave a soft laugh and walked to the large front window. "Must be nice living so close to the boardwalk and the beach."

"It usually is. Nights like tonight can get loud, though. Having thousands of people essentially in your front yard."

"You kind of have no choice but to go to this thing every year then, huh?"

"Yeah, but I've never had a mission before." I rubbed my hands together. "Shall we get going?"

"Yeah. Bring your phone. I figure we'll fan out and look for this guy or his friend. Whoever finds him first can call or text the other."

I gave Gabriel a picture of Billy and Frankie that I'd printed off someone's Facebook page so he'd know who he was looking for. Mom was already out at the fireworks and Perry was still MIA, so I locked up on our way out.

The beach was bustling. There were families, giggling packs of teens, couples on blankets, roving groups of men and women checking each other out. Many I recognized from town, but a good half were tourists. Gabriel and I walked past booth after booth of tantalizing smells: grilled burgers and hot dogs, Italian sausages, pizza, snow cones, ice cream, doughnuts.

Gabriel said, "I could spend the whole night eating."

"Not yet. After I track down Billy Rawlinson you can reward me with some fried dough."

He groaned. "Damn you, voice of reason. OK, let's split up and spread out."

I nodded and broke off to the left, passing the grandstand where the high school band was playing. I tried to act nonchalant while at the same time searching for Billy and Frankie in the sea of faces. I squeezed through a horde of gum-snapping girls I recognized as seniors from my school.

"He did not say that!"

"Yes, he did! And you wouldn't believe what *she* said!"

Please, someone tell me I wouldn't be that annoying if I had girlfriends.

"Sure, you will be."

I whipped around and nearly got a faceful of candyfloss. I moved the purple sugar cloud to the side and glared at my mother. She wore a white, short-sleeved peasant blouse and a patchwork skirt.

"You have to stop listening in on my thoughts without my permission, Mom. It's not cool."

She shoved a piece of candyfloss in my mouth to shut me up. "I didn't do it on purpose, Clarity. I was strolling along listening in to the crowd."

"Pick up anything interesting?"

"Actually, I did. That detective's son can't stop checking out your legs. He loves this little pink dress you've got on. So much so that he's actually mad at himself for it." She shook her head.

I blushed. "Did you happen to pick up anything *important*?"

"Like a man walking along thinking, 'I killed Victoria Happel'?"

"Exactly."

"No such luck. But dear, people don't wander around thinking about their biggest secrets all the time. The killer could be standing right next to me and all I might pick up from him is how he wants to buy some barbecued chicken."

"Have you seen Billy Rawlinson or Frankie Creedon?" I asked.

Distaste turned her mouth down. "No. Why are you looking for those scoundrels?"

"Billy might be a witness in the case. Or a suspect."

"I'll keep my eyes out and my mind open."

"Thanks," I said. "Enjoy invading everyone's privacy."

Mom kissed me on the cheek and wandered off.

People were starting to reserve their spots on the beach for the fireworks. I stumbled through a mass of blankets and beach chairs, mumbling my apologies now and then when I stepped on the edge of a blanket or toe. I heard someone call my name, glanced to the side, and saw Nate ambling towards me. He was scowling, which was very un-Natelike.

"Where's that brother of yours?"

"You haven't seen him today, either?" I asked, feeling a pang of dread.

"No, and he was supposed to meet me so we could come here together, but he stood me up. He's my wingman. How is a shy guy like me supposed to meet a nice girl without my wingman?" Nate smiled, but I frowned. Not only did Perry stand up Mom, but now he'd stood up Nate. This was not my brother. Not the Perry I knew.

I didn't want to let on that something deeper was wrong, so I plastered on a fake smile and offered Nate my arm. "I'll be your wingwoman for a few minutes. Let's walk."

He laughed and circled his arm through mine. We approached the more family-oriented section of the party. A giant bouncy castle seemed to be the most popular attraction, in addition to the carnival-style games where kids could spend twenty of their daddies' dollars to win a stuffed animal worth a buck.

"Have you seen Billy Rawlinson or Frankie Creedon around tonight?" I asked Nate.

Nate scratched his head. "I may have seen Frankie. I'm not sure."

I straightened. "Do you remember where?"

"No, sorry. Sounds important. What's up?"

I wondered how much I was allowed to say. "Ah, nothing really."

He grinned. "So that's how it's going to be."

"What?" I asked innocently.

"You're Miss Big-Time-Help-the-Police-Out and you can't fraternize with your lowly reporter friend any more."

"Got me." I winked.

"How is it working with Officer Yummy anyway?" he said sarcastically.

"Wouldn't you like to know?" I waggled my eyebrows.

Nate suddenly turned from his usual light-hearted self to serious. "Be careful with him, Clare."

I dropped his arm. "What do you mean?"

"There are things about him and his father—"

"Clare," said a voice behind me. Not Nate's, but just as familiar.

"I'll get going," Nate said, backing up. "If you see the dumbass, tell him I'm mad at him for standing me up."

I turned around.

"The dumbass?" Justin asked.

"Yes, you're not the only one in town. Who knew?"

He smiled. Every time I tried to hurt him, he just smiled. I'd have to try harder.

"You look beautiful tonight," he said, looking me up

and down. "You wore that dress on the picnic we took in the spring. Remember, it was the first warm day of the season. . ." His voice trailed off.

"I'd love to wax nostalgic, Justin, but I've got work to do."

I tried to walk away, but he gently grabbed my arm. A love-struck couple frowned as they had to let go of each other's hands to get around us.

"I'm sorry, Clare. I don't know how many times you need me to say it. How many different ways I can try to prove it. But I'm sorry."

"Sorry doesn't change the past."

"I know that, but I was hoping—"

"Hoping what, that we'd get back together? Go back to the way we were? That I could look at you and not think about you with Tiffany?"

A bell rang loudly as a man swung the mallet down on the test-of-strength game. His girlfriend clapped giddily. He handed her his prize, a white teddy bear, and was rewarded with a kiss.

Justin cast his eyes down. "No, I know that's not possible. At this point, I was just hoping that you would stop hating me."

I softened a bit. "You know I don't hate you," I whispered.

The wind blew a lock of hair over my eyes and he

tucked it behind my ear, his fingers lingering for a moment on my neck before dropping. Part of me wanted to forgive him. Part of me longed to go back to the way things were. I was never as happy as when I was with him. I looked up into his deep blue eyes.

"There you are!"

Justin and I stepped away from each other at the resounding boom of Gabriel's voice, like two kids caught in the make-out room.

"What's up?" I asked, pushing the moment with Justin out of my mind.

"I texted you. You didn't write back. I was worried."

Worried? About me? I pulled my phone out of my bag. "Sorry, I didn't hear the tone."

Gabriel looked at Justin. "Hey."

Justin nodded. "Hey."

"Any sign of Billy or Frankie?" I asked Gabriel.

"No." He looked around. "I doubt they'd be hanging around here with the five-year-olds, either. What are you doing?"

Oh, just having an uncomfortably tense and emotional moment with my ex-boyfriend. Nothing much. "Justin stopped me. I'm on my way over there." I pointed to an area of the beach where guys were tossing a football back and forth. "Haven't checked out that side yet."

"OK," Gabriel said. "I'm going to check the toilets." But instead of walking off, he waited, eyes shifting from me to Justin and back.

"I'll let you get back to work," Justin finally said, getting the hint.

The three of us set off in separate directions. I scanned the crowd around a small campfire, my eyes going from face to face through the flickering light of the flame. The guys who were playing football had stopped and were now pulling beers from a cooler. I inched closer to them. The sand was deeper over here, not hard and packed like at the carnival area. I slipped off my sandals and walked with them in my hand. The crowd of guys glanced up at me as I passed. I tried my best to study all their faces without them thinking I was checking them out. No signs of Billy or Frankie. I pushed on, with the sounds of clinking bottles and masculine laughter behind me.

I stepped over a couple on a beach blanket who really needed to get a room. As I averted my eyes, I spotted Stephen Clayworth waving at me. He was flanked on either side by his parents, Cecile and Dallas, sitting as properly as one could in beach chairs. Stephen motioned for me to come over, but I played dumb and kept on walking. I didn't have time for whatever he had to say.

"Clare!"

Man. I stopped and turned around. Undaunted by my ignoring him, Stephen trudged through the sand towards me, completely overdressed in khakis and a dress shirt.

"Wait up," he said as he got closer.

"I'm sorry, Stephen, but I can't stop to talk. I'm looking for someone."

"I'll help you look as we talk, then. How's that?"

"You know Billy Rawlinson or Frankie Creedon?"

"Of course, but why would you—"

I interrupted, "That's who I'm looking for, so if you want to talk you have to keep up and help me look."

"Deal," he said, jumping over someone's blanket to keep up with me. "Listen, I wanted to apologize for my behaviour at the boardwalk. I wasn't myself. I'd been drinking a little."

And I was hearing that excuse an awful lot lately. "Apology accepted."

"It's been a tough year." Then he thunked himself in the forehead. "I bet I'm preaching to the choir."

"What do you mean?" I asked, squinting at some shadows under the boardwalk.

"You've had a tough year, too. It's terrible what Justin did to you." He shook his head. "But getting dumped while giving you a gift like that, that's got to sting." He scoffed. "He sure deserved it, though."

"What are you talking about?"

"Cheating on you."

"No. 'Dumped while giving you a gift like that.' What does that mean?"

Stephen's already sunburned face turned redder in the moonlight. "Oh, I guess he never got to that part. I assumed. . ."

I thought back to the night I'd found out about Justin's betrayal. He'd said he had a surprise for me. But then I'd touched his jacket and everything else had happened so fast.

"What gift?" I asked.

He looked down at the sand and kicked it around a bit with his loafers.

"Stephen," I said sternly, in my best imitation of his mother.

"My father's campaign kind of had a guy. His job was to follow Harry Spellman around in the hopes that he'd screw up and we could get it on video."

I gasped. "Seriously? That's gross."

"It's politics, Clare. All's fair and all that. Plus, it was my dad's idea, not mine." Stephen scratched the back of his neck. "Anyway, our guy followed Harry and Justin into a jewellery store. Justin picked up a promise ring. One he'd had specially made. He had designed it himself."

I suddenly found it hard to breathe. I wanted to sink down into the sand, but couldn't get my knees to bend. That was just like Justin to design the ring himself. He'd probably had it in his pocket when he walked through the door and I'd pulled on his jacket. If I hadn't done that . . . if I hadn't found out about Tiffany . . . I would have jumped up and down at the sight of that ring. It would have been one of the happiest moments of my life. I'd be wearing the ring right now.

"Maybe I shouldn't have said anything," Stephen said, eyeing me worriedly.

"It's OK," I lied. "It's in the past. I'm fine."

He backed up a few steps, probably scared I was going to cry. "I'm going to head back to my parents before the fireworks start. I apologize again for my behaviour last night."

I nodded and waved him off, glad to be alone so I could try to catch my breath.

"What is this, social hour?" Gabriel stormed up to me. "Every time I come to find you, you're gabbing with a different guy. How about doing some work? How about instead of flirting with every dude here, you try to find the guys we came for?"

My head snapped towards him and my eyes must have shot flames because he immediately took a step back.

"Are you OK?" he asked.

"That depends. Are you done with your condescending reprimanding?" Before he could respond I advanced on him, my finger pointing in his face. "For your information, I asked everyone I talked to if they'd seen Billy or Frankie. I figured the more eyes the better. I didn't exactly stop to talk about the weathcr."

He put his hands up in surrender. "I'm sorry! I'm sorry. Chill."

I turned away, my anger dissolving as quickly as it swelled, replaced again with sadness.

Gabriel approached me slowly and put a gentle hand on my shoulder. "Something happened. What?"

"It's personal," I whispered, and shrugged off his hand, despite the little part of me that liked it there.

He waited for a few moments. "I don't think either of those guys we're looking for are here. Between the two of us, we've been up and down the length of the beach. I'm going to call it a night, start fresh at some of the local joints in the morning. They're bound to turn up."

I agreed, said goodbye, and watched Gabriel walk away. But even that pleasurable sight couldn't cheer me up. All I could think about was Justin's face as he'd walked through the door that night. He'd been so happy to see me, with a goofy smile and the surprise in his pocket. My ability had ruined it all.

For a moment, I wondered if it would have been better if I hadn't found out about his betrayal. It was a drunken mistake. He regretted it. It wouldn't happen again. If I was a normal girl, instead of a psychic freak, I wouldn't have got the vision. I would have accepted his promise ring. We'd still be together. I'd be happy.

No, I chided myself.

Justin was the one to blame here. He'd cheated. Even if I hadn't found out the psychic way, Tiffany would surely have told me, to rub it in my face. Nothing would be different. I'd still be here, alone and angry.

I began to walk back home, sticking close to the shadows along the boardwalk in the hopes that I wouldn't be stopped by anyone else who wanted to talk. I was all talked out, all thought out. I just wanted to go to bed.

And that's when an arm snaked around my neck and dragged me backwards and under the boardwalk.

ELEVEN

I clawed at the hairy arm around my neck and dug my heels into the sand, but he was stronger than me and was still able to pull me into the darkness. I wanted to kick him in his two little vulnerables, but couldn't get my leg up that high backwards and ended up flailing at the air. I stopped trying to pull his arm off my neck and simultaneously brought down both of my elbows into his gut. He grunted and let me go.

"Wait," he said, before I had a chance to run. "I wasn't going to hurt you."

Despite the complete darkness surrounding us, I recognized that nasal voice. "Frankie?"

"That's twice in one week I've taken your elbow in my stomach. Jeez, Clare, I didn't mean to scare you."

"Then why did you attack me?"

"I didn't hurt you! I'm the one whose arm is bleeding from those fingernails of yours."

I pulled him out from under the boardwalk so I could see him. His face was unshaven, his hair dishevelled. His eyes darted back and forth.

"What's going on?" I demanded. My breathing returned to normal, but my heart still raced.

Frankie scurried back under the boardwalk, just enough to keep hidden. "I heard you were looking for me. I need to talk to you, but didn't want anyone to see me."

"You idiot. You're lucky I don't have a Taser or Mace on me."

"I said I'm sorry!" His voice trembled. "Why are you looking for me?"

"I'm looking for Billy."

He paused. "So am I."

"You don't know where he is?"

"No. I can't find him anywhere and I'm worried."

"When was the last time you saw him?" I asked. I couldn't believe I was standing here, talking with Frankie about Billy as if either of them were my friends. If Billy didn't hold the key to the case, I wouldn't have cared one ounce about where he was. And Frankie was talking to me like I was a fellow human being for once, instead of mercilessly mocking me. But only because he needed me. He thought I could help.

"Yesterday," he said, rubbing the claw marks I'd left on his arm.

"One day without seeing him, that's nothing to worry about."

Frankie shook his head vigorously. "Something was going on. When I saw him in the morning, he was all smiles. Said he had something big up his sleeve. Something life-changing. But then I called him in the afternoon to see if he'd tell me what this big thing was and he was completely different."

"How so?"

"Scared. Billy doesn't get scared. And now he's gone. I think he ran."

Damn. What did he see that frightened him enough to make him bolt? Did someone threaten him? I thought about Perry, also missing, and hated how these threads were coming together.

"Wouldn't he have told you where he was going?" I asked. "You two are like brothers."

"I dunno. He's not answering his phone. I can't find him anywhere."

"So why are you acting all sketchy, pulling me under the boardwalk to talk to you?"

"I know what everyone in town says." He mimicked a high voice. "'Billy and Frankie share a brain.'"

"So?"

"So whoever scared Billy enough to make him run away might think I'm in on whatever Billy did. I'm staying hidden until he comes back."

"And if he doesn't?" I asked, but a thundering boom muffled my words.

I jumped and twisted around. The night sky lit up with sparkling purple and blue hues, followed by applause and a smattering of "oooh"s and "ahhhh"s. I'd have to bring Frankie somewhere else to continue this conversation if either of us was going to hear a word. I turned back.

Frankie was gone.

I ducked and peeked under the boardwalk but saw only black. I wasn't about to head under there again. So Frankie was free of me.

For now.

I called Gabriel's mobile and quickly relayed the information to him. We made plans to catch up tomorrow. But now, all I wanted was sleep.

I made my way back through the swarms of people, fireworks booming overhead, and by the time I got home the grand finale had ended and most of the crowd were working their way home as well. I trudged up the walk towards the front porch, then stopped.

The outside light was off. *That's weird,* I thought. I never forget to put the light on and I had been the last one to leave. With the entire porch shrouded in darkness, it seemed different, scary. I told myself to grow up and keep walking. I'd probably been so distracted by Gabriel's company that I'd forgotten to put on the light on my way out.

I pulled out my key and squinted at the darkness so I wouldn't trip on the stairs. The wood creaked beneath my feet. Then I heard something else. Steady, deep breathing. I gazed at the shadows along the porch. One shadow in particular on the porch swing. I squinted hard, desperate for enough light to make out what or who it was.

The shadow moved. Slightly, but enough for me to recognize that it was a person. With my key held out before me like a weapon, I yelled, "Get up and tell me what you want!"

"Ahhhhh! Wha? Huh?"

I'd recognize that babbling anywhere. "Perry?"

"Clare?"

I quickly turned my key in the lock, opened the door, and switched on the outside light. The once menacing shadow morphed into the familiar frame of my brother as he sat up.

"What's going on?" he asked.

"I should be asking you that. I was this close to stabbing your eye with my house key. What are you doing sleeping on the porch swing?"

He raked his hands through his hair. "Sorry. When I left this morning, I didn't bring my key. No one was home so I lay down to wait for you or Mom and I must have fallen asleep."

My blood pressure ballooned. "Where have you been all day and night? You missed your readings. Mom's really pissed."

Perry picked at a chip of paint peeling off the swing. "I didn't want her to read my thoughts. To know I was with Vicki the night she was murdered."

I crossed my arms. "You can't stay away from Mom for ever. She'll find out soon enough. She may have already plucked it from *my* mind. Who knows with her."

"You're right." He hung his head. "I'm having a tough time with this. I feel so . . . guilty."

My heart sped up. "About what?"

"Vicki's death. If I hadn't left her alone, maybe I could have saved her."

Survivor's guilt, I thought.

"Or maybe you'd be dead, too." I tried to be supportive and say the right thing, while inside I was wondering if he was telling the truth. I couldn't believe I was thinking like this about my brother.

I gazed up at a moth fluttering against the bright porch light. Then an idea took form. My energy returned as adrenaline kicked in.

Perry stood up slowly. "Anyway, I'm sorry for scaring you. I'm heading upstairs to bed."

"Wait," I said, grabbing his arm. "You can make it up to me."

"How?"

"Come with me to the King's Courtyard, to Victoria's room, and try to contact her."

He blanched.

"She might be able to tell you who killed her and then this nightmare will be over."

Perry agreed, under duress, to come with me. We got to King's Courtyard just before midnight.

"By the way," Perry asked as he drove, "how are you planning on getting into her room?"

I smirked. "I have my ways."

We pulled up to the main office. I told Perry to wait in the car. I hoped that creepy guy was behind the desk. He was, and he recognized me as I walked in, the bell jingling as the door closed behind me.

"What can I do for you?" he asked nervously.

My hopes were that he assumed I was with the cops since I'd been at the crime scene with Gabriel. If so, this would be easier than I thought. I wouldn't even have to bat my eyes or flip my hair.

"I need the key to the room again."

He hesitated, as if it suddenly occurred to him that I might not have the right to be there.

I added, "Gotta get this scene squared away so you can finally have your room back." I flashed a smile, hoping he couldn't sense how nervous I was. I added, "Like you said, those murder groupies will pay you big bucks to stay in there."

He perked up at that and moments later I held the key to room 108 in my hand. I returned to the car where Perry was sweating in the driver's seat.

"Did you get it?"

I dangled the key in front of him. "Never doubt your sister."

We pulled into a spot a few doors down from Victoria's room and made sure no one was watching as we sneaked up to the room and let ourselves in. I bounced from foot to foot, feeling like I'd had three cups of coffee.

"I don't like this," Perry whispered as I shut the door

behind us. He reached for the light switch and I grabbed his hand.

"What?" he asked.

"If we don't want to arouse suspicion, it's best to leave the lights off."

"But it's dark in here. And, you know, the ghost."

"How old are you, eight? There's enough light coming through the blinds. And since when are you afraid of ghosts? You talk to them for a living!"

"Yeah," he said. "Little old ladies who died of geriatric diseases contact me to tell their grandchildren about the money hidden in their knitting baskets. Not murdered girls who I've, you know, slept with!"

"There's a first time for everything." I pushed his shoulders down, urging him to sit on the bed.

He jumped up. "Clare! Not there! That's where she was killed!"

"Shh. Keep your voice down. Fine." I pointed towards the chair in the corner. "Sit there. Just focus and let's do this thing before we get caught in here."

He slumped into the chair and closed his eyes. I'd seen this look on his face a thousand times. Chin to chest. Long, slow breaths. No sound, no movement. He needed complete silence for the deep concentration that was required for his gift to work.

I gazed around the darkened room at the shadows. A chill passed over me and I rubbed my shoulders. Once again, I was glad to have my gift and not Perry's.

But I hoped he was able to summon her. Maybe it could really be this easy. She'd tell us who did it and this would all be over.

Perry sat up straight and his eyes snapped open.

"She's here?" I whispered.

He held his finger up to shush me and slowly panned the room until his eyes stopped in the corner. He stood and inched his way closer.

"I'm sorry for—" he began, then stopped as if interrupted.

It was as if I was eavesdropping on one end of a phone conversation.

Perry moved forward again, pleading with his hands. "Wait. I just want to ask you some questions."

His eyes widened. "That's not true!" He stumbled backwards a few steps. "Please, let me explain."

The temperature dropped, and I could see my quickening breath in the air.

"Wait!" Perry yelled. Then, as if a plug had been pulled, all the energy drained out of the room. Perry sank down to the floor and pulled his knees to his chest.

"She's gone?" I asked.

He nodded. "Doesn't matter. She won't talk to me."

"Why not?"

He looked up at me with sad eyes. The same look he'd given me countless times as a child when he'd broken my toys by playing too rough with them. Remorseful, pleading and ultimately easy to forgive.

"Why won't she talk to you, Perry?"

He looked away. "Because she says I killed her."

TWELVE

That went well. Nothing makes you feel as warm and fuzzy as when the ghost of a murder victim says your brother is her killer. I'd brought Perry to the motel hoping to end this whole thing, clear his name and drag him out of the depression he'd spiralled into. Instead, I'd made it a whole lot worse.

Victoria said he'd killed her. Great. This would be one more secret I was keeping from Justin and Gabriel, and the usually stoic Perry was on his way to a nervous breakdown. At least I convinced him to go back home with me rather than hide somewhere else from Mom.

The next day, I woke early, before my alarm. I should have got up to shower, but instead I was staring at my ceiling as clouds of uncertainty fogged my brain. What if Perry's erratic behaviour wasn't survivor's guilt? What if it wasn't just an *assumption* on Victoria's part that Perry did it? What if it was the truth, staring me in the face, and I was going along for the ride, protecting him? Protecting a murderer.

My brother.

I jerked in surprise at the loud ringtone of my mobile.

I reached over and grabbed it off the nightstand. "Hello?" I croaked.

"Clare?"

"Yeah, Justin."

"Oh, it didn't sound like you."

"This is what I sound like when I get woken up too early." Though it wasn't the phone that had woken me up.

"Scary." He snickered. "Anyways, get up. You've got to come down to the station."

"Why?"

"They have Joel Martelli in custody."

"Victoria's ex-boyfriend?"

"That's the one."

"I'll be there soon."

I sat up and swung my legs over the side of the bed. But before I could stand, the phone rang again in my hand.

"Yeah?"

"One more thing." Justin paused. "Will you have your mother drive you? And, like, bring her in?"

I'm not even going to ask. "Fine."

Before I jumped in the shower, I padded down the hallway to Mom's room to pass on the message about her presence being requested. She was delighted. There's nothing she loves more than feeling needed.

After showering, I swept my tangled mess of curls up into a ponytail and put on a violet sleeveless top and a tan skirt. I wanted to look semi-professional, but there was no way I was wearing trousers in this heat. The casual skirt would do.

As Mom started the car and sped to the station, my thoughts again turned to Perry. Now that I was up and the sunlight had burned away the darkness of the previous night, the doubts returned to their small little corner of my brain and sisterly worry took their place. I hadn't seen him around the house this morning. He hadn't looked good last night after we came home. Who would, considering what had happened. I wondered if he was up yet, but I didn't want to ask Mom and set her off. If worrying about your children were an Olympic sport, she'd get the gold. No need to stir up that storm.

Justin met us at the door to the station and pulled me aside. "Thanks for coming and bringing your mother," he whispered.

"No problem. What's going on?"

"They're putting Joel Martelli in a lineup for the witness."

I knit my brow in confusion. "What witness?"

"Starla Fern."

"My mother didn't see anything."

"No, but she can hear what he's thinking."

My mouth dropped open. "I thought you were bringing us down here for something official."

He shrugged. "Your mother might give them something to go on. Somewhere to start. It's worth a shot. What's your problem?"

"I have two, actually. First, Detective Toscano will never go along with this. Second, now that you've claimed you have a witness, my mother's going to be in the murderer's sights. Thanks, you just placed her in mortal danger."

"It's a one-way mirror. If Joel is the killer, he won't see your mom's face. Nothing to worry about there. And Detective Toscano . . . well, let my father deal with him. This was his idea."

I had to admit I was curious to see if Mom could get anything useful out of Joel. And if she wasn't in danger. . . "OK," I said hesitantly.

Justin stayed in the lobby while Harry Spellman led Mom and me into a small room with concrete walls and a large glass window. I lowered myself into an uncomfortably hard chair and looked around. I'd seen these rooms in movies and on crime TV shows, but never in real life. I peered through the one-way glass at the other side, where the "suspects" would line up, and was surprised by the little thrill I felt in my chest. Working with the police was definitely more exciting than being holed up in our house doing readings for tourists all day.

Mr Spellman had left the room to go tell the doubting detective the plan. The raised voices I heard coming our way were a sure sign that my prediction was spot-on. Anthony Toscano wasn't having it. He burst into the room, startling my mother, who put her hand to her mouth.

"Sorry to frighten you, Ms Fern," Anthony said.

"No problem, Detective." She paused and tilted her head to the side. "And I agree, my daughter and I do look a lot alike."

Anthony's cheeks coloured. He paused, as if reconsidering, then turned to Mr Spellman. "I'll go along with this circus show on one condition."

"What's that?" Mr Spellman asked, crossing his arms.

"Don't tell her which one is our suspect."

"Ah, a test," Mom said.

"There's no need to waste Starla's time by having her listen to the decoys," Mr Spellman said, but Mom interrupted with a touch on his arm.

"That's fine, Harry. I'll do whatever the detective needs me to do. I'll listen in on them all."

Detective Toscano nodded and poked his head into the hallway. "Bring them in!"

A parade of five guys marched into the room on the other side of the glass and followed orders to face the mirror. They were all a little under six feet tall and skinny, with short haircuts. One in particular was good-looking, in a bad-boy kind of way, with spiky hair, pierced ears, and tattoos down his arms.

Mom walked slowly across the room, stopping now and then to close her eyes and purse her lips. After several minutes, she sat. "I can rule out number two."

Number two was the good-looking bad boy, and from the look Gabriel and his father shared, I guessed he was Joel Martelli.

"You can only rule out one of them?" Detective Toscano asked, with an annoying I-knew-it tone.

Mom gave him an icy stare. "I can't flip through their memories. I can only hear what they're thinking right now. So if the murderer was thinking, 'Yeah, I killed her. I did it and I'm going to do it again,' right now, then I'd hear it. But none of them are thinking that."

"Then why did you rule out number two?"

"He's terrified because he stole a car and he thinks he's going to be charged for that."

"So?" Anthony said.

Mom sighed. "If you murdered someone and stole a car, which crime would you be more worried about getting fingered for while standing in a lineup?"

"What about the others? Anything from them?" Mr Spellman asked.

"Nothing interesting. Though number four thinks Detective Toscano has a cute rear end."

Detective Toscano blushed and left the room, mumbling about a waste of his time. Mr Spellman thanked us for coming and told us we could go.

"I'm sorry I couldn't do more to help," Mom told me.

I waved her off. "You did great, Mom."

I wished she had got something we could use from Joel. Most of all so we could close the case, get the killer behind bars, and help ease Perry's mind. But secondly to shove it in Gabriel's face that he was wrong about my family and shouldn't have doubted us.

On our way out, we walked by Detective Toscano hunched over another officer's desk. They were talking in hushed tones, but I picked up what he was telling the officer to do. Run the plates of the car Joel Martelli was driving.

Maybe my wish wasn't so far off.

THIRTEEN

"I really thought he was guilty," I said, pouting as we climbed the stairs and walked in the front door of the house.

"Don't worry." Mom patted my shoulder. "Detective Toscano will find the real killer. He's a spitfire, that one. He's not going to give up until he gets what he wants. Oh, hello, dear," Mom said.

Perry was standing outside the reading room, his face pale, eyes sunken. I guessed sleep still wasn't gracing him with its presence, either.

"We have a walk-in," he said. "But I don't feel well enough. I can't." His voice cracked.

"No worries," I jumped in. "Gabriel doesn't need me for anything that I know of today. I can work. Go upstairs to bed." I shuffled Perry towards the staircase, wanting him to get out of Mom's range ASAP.

"You don't mind, honey?" Mom asked me.

"Not at all." I entered the reading room and found our customers, two handsome middle-aged men. I did my usual introduction, welcoming them to the Fern family home.

They exchanged a look and grinned at me. "Sorry," the blond one said. "We didn't expect you to look so. . ."

"Frankly," the dark-haired guy picked up, "we thought you'd be an old hag."

"Oh, that's my mother."

Their eyes widened as Mom came in on the heels of that line and then we all had a good laugh. The reading went smoothly. Mom awed them with her telepathic skills and I impressed them by relaying details of their past vacations together to the Cape and even the day they met. They paid and left happy and entertained. If only every reading went that way.

I was about to make a sandwich in the kitchen when I heard the bell ring, signalling another customer. Busy day. Mom would be happy and maybe stop obsessing about Madame Maslov.

I returned the plate to the cabinet and backtracked to the foyer. "Oh, it's you."

"You sound disappointed," Nate said. He wore cargo shorts and a green polo shirt that brought out his eyes.

"I was hoping for a paying customer, but I'm always

delighted to see the Nate-ster." I gave him a playful punch on the arm.

He smiled. "That's what I like to hear. Is Perry home? I want to drag him to lunch."

"He's sleeping. He doesn't feel well." Nate's face filled with concern so I quickly added, "I was just about to make a sandwich, but I'd be happy to accompany you to the world-class five-star establishment known as Yummy's. If you'll have me."

He brightened immediately. "Perry should get sick more often! Let's roll."

A half hour later, my belly delighting in the first of many French fries, I leaned back and smiled. I didn't even mind that we'd got stuck with the booth that had three duct-tape repairs on the cushion. "This is good. I needed this today."

"Having a tough time working with Detective Delicious?" Nate smirked.

"The wannabe detective is delicious to *look* at. But frustrating to work with." I stopped to munch another fry. "The case is getting to me. I thought we had the guy, but it looks like we were wrong. How about you? Hear anything around the newsroom?"

He shook his head. "Nothing solid. Just rumours and talk."

"What kind of talk?"

He paused. "The kind you don't want to hear."

I leaned forward. "Nate Garrick, you've known me since I was a little girl. You know you can't tease me like that. Spill."

He spoke softly, almost embarrassed to say the words. "I've heard a couple people suggesting the mayor."

"Mr Spellman?" I yelled. *Justin's dad?* I thought. No way.

"Shhh. Keep your voice down."

I leaned back and crossed my arms. "What motive would he have to kill some random tourist?"

"So the town would see him as a hero. Kill one disposable tourist, someone who's single, with no kids. Then arrest someone for the murder, saving the town and its people, who will be so grateful they'll re-elect him in record numbers on election day."

"Munchausen mayor? That's ridiculous."

"Crazier things have happened. Plus, isn't it quite a coincidence that he brought in this new hotshot detective a week before the murder?"

The idea was so ludicrous I hardly knew what to say. "That's . . . that's . . . crazy talk!"

Nate shrugged. "Maybe Detective Toscano's involved, then. He has a shady past."

"What do you mean?" I took a bite of my sandwich.

"My boss assigned me a fluff piece. Introducing the new detective to the small town. You know, light stuff. But I've been doing background on him and it's not so fluffy. He didn't leave New York City on his own terms."

I took a sip of my drink. "He was pushed out?"

"That's what I'm hearing."

"Again, Nate, it's just talk, no solid evidence. This summer job better not turn you into a gossipmonger."

He rolled his eyes. "Yeah, I'm going to be Eastport's Perez Hilton. This is how the business works, Clare. Believe me. We have one reporter following up on a possible Mayor Spellman mistress and another reporter investigating a possible Dallas Clayworth mistress. Sometimes rumours are just rumours, but sometimes they lead to the truth."

I made a face. "It all seems so seedy to me."

He fiddled with a rip in the paper placemat. "Just be on the safe side, Clare. Don't trust the Toscanos. They're hiding something. I know it. Don't get too close. At least not until I get some answers."

I knew Nate was ambitious, but it seemed to me that he was taking this story personally. Before I could ask him more, my mobile rang. I looked at the caller ID. Gabriel.

"What's up?" I said, answering.

"Where are you?" he asked.

"At Yummy's, getting lunch."

"I'll pick you up outside in five minutes."

"OK, where are we going?"

"Twenty-six Berkshire Drive. Billy Rawlinson's parents' home."

"OK, see you in five."

Refusing to meet Nate's eyes, I said, "That was Gabriel. I've got to go meet him."

Nate nodded and reached for his wallet. I pulled some bills out of my pocket and slid them on to the table. "This one's on me. You get it next time."

Nate had a look on his face that I couldn't figure out.

"I don't mean to tell you what to do," he said. "You know I'm only looking out for you, right?"

"I know. I've always felt I had two brothers instead of one." I kissed his cheek and headed out.

Betty and Herbert Rawlinson lived in a split-level home on a road with other split-level homes that varied only by colour and lawn ornament selection. Berkshire Drive was probably pretty sweet when all the homes were new and hip in 1970, but now it seemed as dated as an episode of *The Brady Bunch*. The Rawlinsons' house was painted an interesting shade of baby blue, which may have looked nice on the paint can, but translated into a garishly bright colour on the wood shingles.

Gabriel told me he'd asked his father to accompany us to make it official, but the detective had refused. So this wasn't police business. Two friends from school were going to show up at the house, looking for Billy.

That would be us.

We'd formulated a plan on the way over. Thankfully, the Rawlinsons had never come to my house for a reading. I'd never met them and they wouldn't know I was the girl their son had bullied for years. The plan hinged on this, since I was pretending to be Billy's friend.

Gabriel knocked on the door and Betty Rawlinson quickly answered.

"Good afternoon, Mrs Rawlinson. Billy wouldn't happen to be here, would he?" Gabriel asked.

Betty smiled. Probably thinking what a polite and handsome young man Gabriel was, when he was really lying through his perfectly straight teeth.

"Are you friends of his?" she asked.

"Yes," I said. "But we can't seem to find him anywhere. He's not at the motel."

"He's not here, either," she said, "but please come on in."

She led us up the stairs to the dining room. The table was piled high with laundry.

Betty swept all the clothing into a basket. "Sorry, I was doing some folding when you arrived."

"No need to clean up for us, ma'am," Gabriel said. "We're sorry to barge in on you like this, but to be honest we're a little bit worried."

"We were with Billy last week," I said. "He borrowed a bunch of my DVDs and we were supposed to meet him Saturday night to get them back. He wasn't around. And we haven't been able to find him. I wondered if maybe he was sick and decided to come home for a few days."

"I wish that were the case." Betty sat down at the table and motioned for us to do the same. "His father and I have been looking for him, too."

"When was the last time you saw him?" Gabriel asked.

"He came home Saturday night," Betty said and cleared her throat. "It was kind of strange because it was the middle of the night. I don't know exactly what time. I heard noises. Herbert got his baseball bat and followed the sound to Billy's room. He was in there sitting at his desk. He looked shaken up."

"Did he say why?" I asked.

"He said the neighbours were being too noisy at the motel so he was going to spend the night here. When I got up Sunday morning, he was gone and I haven't seen him since. We've been calling his mobile but it goes to voicemail. He usually stops by or calls us every day so it's unusual."

Gabriel and I shared a look before he continued. "Is anything missing from the house? A lot of his clothing or anything to suggest he went on a trip?"

She shrugged. "He took his truck."

"The grey one?" I said, and she nodded.

"We'll keep looking around, see if we can find him," Gabriel offered.

Betty reached out and patted his hand. "Tell him to call me right away, OK?"

"We will," I said and rose.

"Do you want to take a quick look in his room to see if your DVDs are in there?" she asked. "I feel bad that he didn't get them back to you when he said he would."

"If it's not too much trouble," I said, holding back my excitement.

"Not at all." Betty rose and led us down the hallway to Billy's room. It was sparsely furnished, with a bed and a desk. A poster featuring a wet, bikini-clad model hung on the wall beside his bed, probably in the same spot for years.

"Have a look," Betty said, backing out of the room.

After she took a few steps down the hallway, Gabriel whispered, "Let's do this. I'll watch for her while you . . . do whatever it is you do. Just do it quick."

Despite Gabriel's order, I moved slowly about the room. Billy Rawlinson's bedroom was the last place I ever thought I'd be. He'd hunted me through the halls of school like a lion to prey. I didn't know if he truly did hate me because of my weird abilities or if he bullied me merely because he thought I was easy to pick on. But now I was in his bedroom, hunting him.

I opened the closet and let my fingers graze over the few items of clothing hanging within. I tried doorknobs, his pillow, the bedspread. Then I moved to the desk and let my hands wander. Nothing. A ratty old T-shirt was strewn over the desk chair. I rested my weight on the chair, my hands gripping the back in frustration. I closed my eyes and kept my mind still and open.

Sometimes it comes slow. Sometimes all at once. And sometimes not at all. This time the vision I least wanted to see rushed to the surface first. I saw bodies writhing, heard moans of pleasure. The vision was small, as if from a distance, with a black halo surrounding it. Then it hit me. I was watching as Billy had watched. Through the hole in his motel room floor.

I was watching my brother and Victoria go at it.

I let go of the shirt and the chair, pushing myself backwards. My eyes snapped open.

"What is it?" Gabriel asked. "What did you get?"

I shook my head, wanting to clear any remnants of the scene out of my mind. "Nothing."

His eyebrows rose. "Nothing? You got nothing from that?"

"Sorry," I snapped. "This isn't a drive-through. You can't just place a psychic order, supersized."

Gabriel held his hands up. "No, I wasn't criticizing you. It really seemed like you got something."

"Not yet," I lied, and quickly went back to work searching for anything else to give Gabriel so I wouldn't have to give him the only truth I had.

"His mother said he'd been sitting at his desk that night," Gabriel said. "Maybe feel the items on the desktop."

Finally, he had a good suggestion. I felt the stack of magazines, a couple bills, and got nothing until I picked up an ordinary pen. Immediately, I saw Billy writing something. I felt his heart racing. This was something important.

"He wrote something," I said. I looked around and saw a small white message pad. "On that. He wrote something on that."

"Let's hope he bore down hard," Gabriel said, fishing a pencil out of a drawer. He held the pencil at a slight angle and gently shaded the top sheet of paper on the pad until, faintly, words could be read. The words Billy wrote on the top sheet that had been torn off. Three words.

I saw you.

FOURTEEN

"'I saw you,'" I read out loud. "What is that? A threat?"

"Sounds like it."

The question I most wanted answered was, "Who?" Who did Billy see? Did he merely see Perry and Victoria messing around or did he see the killer? If Perry had got a note like that, he would have told me, right?

"The note must have gone to the killer," I said.

"Why play around? Why not come to the police?" Gabriel rubbed his chin. "He must have been angling for something. A little blackmail to keep quiet."

"So where is he now? Did he get enough money to leave town? Or did he chicken out and run?"

"We're done here, let's go," Gabriel said, interrupting my stream of thought.

We exchanged polite goodbyes with Betty, then headed towards Gabriel's red Jeep in the driveway.

"What now?" I asked.

"I might have a way to find him," Gabriel said, leaning against the hood. "The pings."

I put up a hand to shield my eyes from the sun reflecting off the windshield. "The what?"

"Billy's mother mentioned his mobile. How mobile phones work is they emit signals called *pings* every few minutes to the closest cellular tower, and the tower relays the info to the network."

"Do the phone companies keep the data?"

"Some just keep the last ping, some keep twenty-four hours' worth. And of course the phone has to be turned on to be pinging in the first place."

"Then call the company and let's see what they've got," I said.

"Not so fast. You need a warrant for that." He unlocked the car. "Maybe my father can get one. We'll see."

By the time I got back home, it was nearly five o'clock. I had to admit, I liked being able to come and go as I pleased. The house was usually attached to me like a ball and chain. Mom always wanted Perry and me there as much as possible in case walk-ins stopped by. Especially during the summer season, the time I most wanted to be outside. This helping the cops gig was giving me a taste of freedom and I liked it.

Gabriel dropped me off and sped away. I wandered up the pavement as a customer left the house. As he got closer, I realized it wasn't a customer after all. It was Phil Tisdell, plodding down the walkway with his shoulders hunched over and his eyes locked on the concrete in fierce concentration.

"Mr Town Clerk!" I greeted him with a smile. "How's it going?"

He gave me a half-hearted wave. "Hi, Clare. See you tomorrow night."

I'd never seen Phil so downtrodden. Normally, he'd give Santa a run for his money in a contest of joviality. Rather than his usual rumpled attire, he wore a neatly pressed blue shirt and dress trousers. And was he wearing cologne?

"What do you mean, tomorrow night?" I asked, his words suddenly sinking in.

"The banquet?"

I shrugged. "You got me."

This answer seemed to depress him further. He sighed. "The Eastport Chamber of Commerce Annual Banquet. It's tomorrow night. Starla said you were accompanying her."

Then, I got it. He'd asked Mom out. And she'd refused him, using me in her lie. I was going to strangle her. But not before I continued her tall tale.

"Oh, that! I didn't realize it was a fancy banquet. I thought it was just a little meeting. Do I have to wear a dress? Mom didn't tell me I'd have to dress up."

The lie came easily and I didn't even have to fake my angry face. I didn't know if Phil bought it or not, but he mumbled something about seeing me there before he shuffled off. I stormed up the front steps and into the house.

"Mom!"

"No need to yell, dear." Mom came out of the kitchen wearing a dress that looked like it'd been created when a sewing machine threw up. "What's the emergency?"

"Did you make that yourself?" I asked, motioning to the abominable creation.

Mom twirled. "Yes, I did. It's called a tapestry sundress. I'm thinking about making more and selling them online. What's all this yelling about?"

"I just saw Phil Tisdell outside."

"Oh." She scooted past me and back into the kitchen. I followed. She wasn't getting out of this one that easily.

Our kitchen was relatively modern for such an old house. We'd remodelled it a few years back and put in an island and new stainless steel appliances. Mom insisted on painting the cabinets bright yellow because the kitchen was "her happy place".

She stood on her tiptoes and pulled a large bowl from one of the happy cabinets now. "I'm making couscous. You want some?"

"No," I said. I didn't even know what that was. "You lied to him, Mom."

She rifled through a drawer looking for something. "Would you rather I hurt his feelings?"

"And you involved me in your lie. So now I have to go to the banquet with you to avoid hurting him further."

She continued to rummage through drawers to avoid eye contact. "Is it that horrible to spend a night with your own mother?"

"That's not the point, Mom." I steeled myself for the next comment. One I'd been holding in for a while. "You can't spend your life avoiding interested men."

She looked up sharply. "What does that mean?"

"What's wrong with Phil?"

"Nothing's wrong with Phil."

"Exactly. He's friendly. He's kind. He's head-over-heels crazy about you. He's cute for an old dude. Bald is sexy these days."

"Clarity, Phil is all those things and if I were interested

in dating anyone, I would definitely date Phil. He's a wonderful man. But you know how things are."

"No, I don't. Explain them to me."

"I don't want to talk about this any more." She bent over her cookbook, pretending to read.

"You're still waiting for Dad to come home."

"Can you get me the bag of flour from the top shelf of the cabinet? You're a tad taller than me."

Inside, I was trembling, knowing I was coming close to a line I'd never crossed before. I stepped up to her and gently lifted her chin with my hand, forcing her to look into my eyes. "It's been fifteen years, Mom," I said, in a soft but insistent tone. "He's not coming home. Dad's never coming home. We don't even know if he's alive."

I thought I'd frozen her with my touch, for she didn't move, didn't breathe, even when I let go of her face. Then a single tear escaped from her eye and she ran past me and out of the room.

Nice going. Now I'd have to buy her flowers for our big date tomorrow night.

The next morning I woke, stretched, and padded across my bedroom rug to the window. I lifted the sash and took a deep breath. You didn't have to be psychic to know a storm was on the way. The air was humid, the sky dark.

I checked my phone. The only word from Gabriel was a text message saying his father got the warrant. There was nothing I could do in the meantime while we were waiting for the phone company, so I figured I'd shower and see if we had any appointments.

Thirty minutes later, I went downstairs and found Mom polishing the long mahogany table in the reading room. We hadn't spoken since our argument and I knew we weren't going to pick up where we left off. Mom preferred to handle difficult conversations by moving forward and pretending they'd never happened.

"Prepping for an appointment?" I asked, leaning against the doorway.

She shook her head. "Wishful thinking. Our first appointment for the day is at eleven. Maybe we'll have an early morning walk-in if someone's disappointed with the wait time at Madame Maslov's."

I gave her shoulder a gentle squeeze. "Business will pick up again. Remember what you always say? Word of mouth is the number one form of advertising in our line of work. As soon as word gets around that none of her so-called predictions come true, people will come back to us."

Mom half smiled, but I knew it was forced. I wished I hadn't said those words about Dad yesterday. She didn't need that on top of her business worries.

"Get your brother up for me, will you? He's been so lazy this week."

If she only knew the half of it.

I headed upstairs. Mom's room was the master bedroom at the end of the hall. Perry's room and mine were opposite each other.

I was thinking up cruel and unusual ways to wake my brother when I heard the shower start. Damn, already up. I went into his room figuring I'd tool around until he was done. The place was a mess. Clothes strewn across the floor. A few crumb-littered plates stacked on his nightstand. An empty plastic water bottle on the floor. I had no intentions of snooping. I just wanted to clean up a bit. I picked up a stack of books from the floor, intending to line them up on the shelf above his desk. A sheet of paper fluttered from the bottom of the pile and slid under the bed. I got down on my hands and knees, pulled it out, and gasped.

Victoria Happel smiled up at me.

She seemed legitimately happy in the picture. A glass raised high as if in mid-toast, her dark eyes looking somewhere off to the left, her face bright. She was smiling radiantly, perhaps about to break into laughter. This moment in time snapped by someone's camera made her more real to me than the grainy newspaper photo or the shadowy naked figure in my visions. My heart went out to her. Betrayed by her boyfriend and her best friend, she'd gone on vacation alone to forget her problems, and ended up dead.

Above the photograph was a headline written in large script that read: *Did you see this woman Saturday night?* In smaller letters beneath the picture were instructions to contact the local police department if you had any information. But this didn't seem like a flyer the police would put together. It wasn't done on a computer, for one. It was handwritten, the picture plopped on top, and then photocopied. Someone had gone through the trouble to do this themselves.

"What are you doing?"

Startled, I fell from my kneeling position back on my butt and the flyer whisked away and landed on Perry's bare feet. He had a towel wrapped around his waist, his hair dripping wet.

"I was going to clean up and found—"

"You were searching my room."

"No! I picked up the stack of books and that fell out."

"It doesn't matter. Whatever. I have to get dressed." He aimed a thumb at the door, a polite way of saying it was time for me to get out.

I stood up and brushed myself off. "Did you make that flyer?"

"No. I found it tacked to a telephone pole near Yummy's."

I cocked my head to the side. "Why did you pull it down?"

"Someone might come forward claiming they saw me leave with her."

"Or someone might come forward with information leading to the real killer," I said.

He looked down at the floor. "I didn't think of that."

"How come I haven't seen these anywhere? Is this the only one you saw?"

His eyes snapped up to mine, glowing with guilt.

"Wait." I thought for a moment. "The night of the fireworks, when you were missing all day. You went around town and took them all down."

He lumbered over to his bed and sat down on the edge. Confession time. "Yeah, I did."

"Do you realize how suspicious that would look if someone saw you doing that?"

"I was careful."

I groaned. "Perry, I'm trying to help you here but you keep digging yourself in deeper." I was frustrated at him. But I was also frustrated by the fact that every time I thought I'd banished any doubts about Perry's innocence, something happened to make me doubt him again.

He propped his elbows on his knees and rubbed his face with his hands. "I guess I wasn't thinking straight. I'm sorry."

My mobile rang. I glanced at the caller ID. "Fine. This is Gabriel anyway. I'll see you later. Try not to make yourself an even more conspicuous suspect while I'm gone."

I closed his door behind me. I flipped open the phone, hoping all that ping talk had amounted to something and they'd tracked Billy down.

At first I heard only static, then a few words. "Woods . . . need you here. Will come get you."

"What?" I pressed the phone harder to my ear as if that would help. "I didn't get that."

"They found him," Gabriel yelled.

"Billy? What's he saying?"

"Not much. He's dead."

FIFTEEN

Of course the storm clouds chose the moment I left the house to open up and start spitting. I ran to Gabriel's Jeep. Thankfully, he had the cover on. Rain began to sprinkle on the windshield. He turned on the wipers, and I winced at their initial squeaking.

During the drive, Gabriel explained that the phone company tracked the pings from Billy Rawlinson's mobile to the state park. Considering the acres of woods and hiking trails, it could have taken days to comb through the entire area. But instead Billy was in the first place they looked – the dirt road that cut through the centre of the park.

Big fat raindrops plunked on the windshield. Moments later a flash of lightning lit up the sky, followed by distant thunder. By the time we reached the park, the rain was coming down so hard it was difficult to see out of the window. Gabriel turned right at the entrance to the service road. He took the dirt road slowly and pulled over behind a single police car. The shadow of a man was in the driver's seat.

"Is that your father?" I asked.

"Yeah. Everyone else is done and gone. Dad promised to look the other way for five minutes. He'll call the coroner to the scene after you're done."

"You mean . . . Billy's still in the truck?"

"Yeah," he said, and grimaced.

I'd never seen a dead body before. And despite the somewhat morbid nature of my family business, the idea of it freaked me out. I swallowed the fear rising in my throat and forced it down. I focused on the strength hidden beneath and coaxed it to the surface. After a few deep breaths, I straightened, full of resolution.

Billy's grey truck was blocking the road. The heavy rain couldn't have been good for the crime scene. My skills were needed even more now. I took a deep breath, grabbed my umbrella, and headed out into the storm.

Gabriel took me by the elbow and led me through the mud. "We don't have much to go on. The rain washed away any tracks or footprints. We don't even know if there was another vehicle or not. No murder weapon. No signs of struggle. After the autopsy, they'll compare the bullet to the one from the first victim. Other than that…" His voice trailed off.

"I'll see what I can do," I said, stepping gingerly up to the truck.

Billy was seated in the driver's seat. I was no medical examiner, but I'd say the cause of death was the bullet hole in his forehead.

Despite having never seen a real dead body, I'd seen plenty on TV, and surprisingly that's what Billy looked like. An actor playing someone dead. Except I knew this was real. He was no actor. He was someone I'd known almost my whole life. Someone I'd hated. I was sure there were moments along the way when his taunting had got so bad that I wished him dead. But looking at him now, I wasn't happy. I was sad. Sad for his parents. Hell, even sad for Frankie.

I turned and handed my umbrella to Gabriel, who stood solemnly behind me, watching with serious eyes.

Slowly, I walked around to the passenger side of the car and got in. Concentrating was difficult. I had to force the thought that I was sitting beside a corpse out of my head. I put my hands in all the places a passenger would: seat belt, the cracked leather interior, the dash. Nothing.

"I don't believe he had a passenger," I said out the open door to Gabriel.

Increasingly frustrated, I returned to the driver's side and explored there, doing my best to ignore Billy. Nothing relevant came until I leaned over the body and placed my hands at ten and two on the steering wheel and then . . . whoosh.

"I see Billy driving," I whispered to Gabriel, who was standing behind me, peering over my shoulder.

"On this road?" he asked.

"I can't tell. It's hazy. But his thoughts are clear."

"What are they?"

I squeezed my eyes tight, tried to hold on to the vision for as long as I could. "Anticipation and fear. He thinks he might be getting something good, but there's an equal chance his plan could backfire."

I stayed silent while I focused.

"What now?" Gabriel asked. "What's he thinking?"

"About his parents. How he's let them down because he didn't amount to anything."

The vision dissolved. I let go of the wheel and stepped back. My racing heartbeat started to slow. "What do you think this means?"

Gabriel rubbed his chin. "I think he was going to try to blackmail the killer. And the killer took the matter into his own hands and shut Billy up for good."

The rain lightened slightly, but a thick mist had settled

in the woods, giving them an eerie glow. Anything or anyone could be hiding in the grey spaces between the trees.

A twig snapped in the forest behind us. Gabriel spun around and squinted at the trees, then turned back to me and shrugged.

"Our time's up," he said. "We should get going."

Then another snap came, not as loud this time, but was quickly followed by a shuffling sound. A chill seeped into my bones.

"Someone's out there," Gabriel said, and he took off into the woods.

I followed, blindly, my hands out in front of me to protect myself from running head first into a tree. The mist made it difficult to see too far ahead, and soon I'd lost Gabriel completely. I didn't want to go deeper into the woods by myself, so I backtracked towards the dirt road where the truck was. Once the truck was in view, the rain picked up again, lashing at my face. I kept my eyes on the ground so I wouldn't trip over a root or fallen branch.

Then I stopped. A footprint was at the base of a tree, but it was quickly eroding in the rain.

Had a person been there minutes ago? Hiding behind the tree? Peeking around it?

I stretched out my fingers and pressed my hand on the trunk of the tree. The bark felt a bit slimy from all the rain. I closed my eyes and concentrated. A moment later, a vision floated to the surface. It shimmered as if I were watching it through a sheet of water. I focused harder and it cleared a bit. Then I gasped.

I was watching myself.

I saw myself lean into the truck and put my hands on the steering wheel.

I shuddered involuntarily and the vision vanished. I yanked my hand from the tree as if it were something disgusting.

Someone had been watching me. And whoever it was knew I was involved in the case now.

I heard panting behind me and spun around. Gabriel skidded to a stop and leaned over to catch his breath. "I ran all around and couldn't find anyone. Maybe it was my dad taking a smoke break."

"Your dad wouldn't run from us."

I thought about relaying my vision to him, but didn't see the point. The person was long gone. If Gabriel didn't believe me and made some snarky remark, we'd fight again. If he did believe me, he might think it was unsafe for me to continue helping with the investigation. And I wasn't giving this up. My brother's life depended on it.

"Or you know what?" Gabriel continued. "It was probably an animal. Yeah, a deer."

Or a hunter, I thought.

The Eastport Chamber of Commerce Annual Banquet was mostly an excuse for local businessmen to pat each other on the backs and for their wives to dress up and gossip. Mom and I arrived fashionably late. I wore a simple black cocktail dress. Mom had on a white embroidered dress that wasn't too bad considering what else lurked in her closet. She immediately began mingling, probably hoping to score some dirt on Madame Maslov. I took to my seat and hid behind a large glass of water with lemon.

"Join you?"

I glanced up nervously, then smiled at Nate. He looked all mature in his striped shirt and khaki trousers. "Sure."

He sat next to me, placing his little notebook on the table next to his drink.

"Ah, you're the lucky one who got assigned to cover this delightful evening."

He grinned. "The real reporters get the big stories, the intern gets the Chamber of Commerce banquet. Why aren't you out there being a socialite like Starla?"

I peeked over his shoulder at the dance floor and saw

Mom and Milly twisting to the music of the live band. "I'd rather keep my seat warm all night."

"What's Perry up to tonight?"

"I don't know. I haven't talked to him."

Nate paused, turning his Coke in his hands. "He seems distant lately."

"Something to drink?" an annoyingly familiar voice asked.

Tiffany bent over and placed cocktail napkins on our table, her twins busting out of her low-cut scoop-neck shirt, leaving little to the imagination. Nate didn't move his eyes from mine, causing Tiffany to frown. Her little display was all for nothing.

"What are you doing here?" I asked her.

"I'm friends with the caterer. Helping him out."

"You? Doing a little something on the side? Nah."

She glared at me and moved on.

"I hope you didn't want another drink," I said to Nate and smirked.

Nate shrugged. "I can hoof it to the bar myself. So, about Perry."

I shook my head. "Who knows. Maybe he needs some of that," I joked, motioning to Tiffany as she walked away.

"He's already had some of that."

I nearly spat out my water. "Perry hooked up with Tiffany?"

"At a party a few months ago."

I felt sick. I didn't know who I was more disgusted by – Tiffany or Perry. He never shared the names and details of his hookups with me, thankfully, because I didn't want to hear it. But this is one I feel he could have given me the heads-up about. Maybe he was embarrassed. Maybe he figured I didn't want to know. Or maybe he just enjoyed keeping secrets.

Nate tipped his Coke back and took a long chug. "Perry's messed around with a lot of chicks he should be ashamed of, but she's the worst of the bunch. She's the one he wishes he could take back."

"Why's that?"

"Tiffany went a little cuckoo after Perry never called her again. Mild stalking, that sort of thing."

And then she purposefully went after Justin, I thought. This whole time I'd assumed she'd done it as the highlight of her lifelong plan to torment me. But maybe this action was different. Maybe she did what she did because hurting me was the best way to hurt my brother.

Nate continued, "Perry stuck with tourists from that point on."

"They're easier to hide from," I said bitterly.

Nate shrugged. "They know it's just a temporary deal. They're here on vacation with their family or maybe they're college girls looking for a good time. But they're only here for a little while. So that's that, maybe see you next summer."

"Why don't you ever join in on the fun?"

"That's not my idea of fun. I'm looking for the real thing."

I plucked at a lint ball on the tablecloth. "I think that's what Perry needs, too. Someone stable to keep him out of trouble."

"He's in trouble?" Nate leaned forward.

I looked into his concerned eyes. If I could trust anyone with this information, it was Perry's best friend.

"The murdered girl," I began slowly.

"Victoria Happel?"

"Yeah. Perry slept with her the night she died."

Nate rocked back in his chair. "No way."

I lowered my voice. "Obviously you can't share this with anyone. Don't even tell Perry I told you. No one can know he was there because then he'll become the top suspect."

"Does he know anything about the murder?"

"No. When he left the motel room, she was alive. But this is why he's so depressed. He feels guilty. Like if he had stayed, he could have saved her."

"Or maybe he'd be dead, too," Nate said, and I nodded.

I nervously twisted and untwisted a strand of hair around my finger as I held back the other information. How Perry had taken down the posters all over town. How Victoria had said Perry was the one who killed her. How Perry's erratic behaviour had even me wondering.

Milly plopped down into the open chair next to me. "Did you see me out there cuttin' a rug on the dance floor? Ol' Milly's still got it." She lifted her dress a few inches and kicked her skinny legs. "Like a Rockette, I am!"

Nate laughed uneasily. "On that note, I'm heading to the bar for another drink. Need anything, ladies?"

Milly asked for an ice water. I told him I was all set.

Milly started babbling about the old days and all the dances she went to. I quickly realized I could be stuck in this conversation all night if I didn't find a way out.

"Hi, Clare," Stephen Clayworth called out as he walked past. He wore a navy blazer with some kind of crest on the pocket.

Jumping out of my seat, I said, "Stephen, I need to talk to you."

He stopped, looking surprised. "About what?"

I took him by the elbow and led him a bit away from the table. "I needed to get out of a certain conversation."

"Ah, so you used me."

I smiled sheepishly. "Sorry."

"I don't mind." He glanced over at the table where his parents were seated. Dallas Clayworth shook a man's hand while Cecile smiled Stepfordly. "It's a welcome break from all the politics talk and brown-nosing for votes going on over there."

In all the chaos of the case and my worrying about Perry, I'd forgotten there was a campaign going on. Stephen couldn't forget, though. That was his life. I was surprised to hear him speak negatively of it.

"Don't you love that stuff, though? It's in your blood, right?" I asked.

"I know politics is where I'll end up ... but that's my future. For now, I'm kind of sick of it all. I leave for college in two months. I think the distance from my parents will do me some good."

Well, colour me impressed. Stephen was a little deeper than I gave him credit for. And he seemed to have dropped his grudge against me for the whole test cheating scandal.

"Well, it was nice talking to you," he said, starting to walk off.

I put my hand on his arm to stop him from leaving. "Stephen?"

He turned. "Yeah?"

I swallowed hard. "Why don't you hate me?"

"What?"

"For telling on you. About the test."

He shrugged. "I was mad at first, but it all worked out fine. And I guess I understand why you did it. I messed with your brother, so you messed with me. Family loyalty. I respect that."

The band finished up the song and announced they'd be back later.

"And that's my cue to go back to my family. Dad's doing a speech," Stephen said. "I've got to go."

I held up the closest wall while boring men did boring speeches. Mom sidled up to me with a champagne flute in her hand. "I know, isn't it disgusting?" she whispered conspiratorially in my ear.

"What?"

She motioned with her head to the table behind her. I glanced over her shoulder and saw Phil Tisdell and a woman seated next to each other. She wore a purple fitted kimono dress and her black hair was held up in a clip. Her face was angular and hard, not that pretty. I realized it was Madam Maslov. Her newspaper ad had included a photo, but this was the first time I was seeing her in real life. Phil whispered something in her ear, and she threw her head back in laughter.

"She cackles like a damned witch," Mom said.

"You're jealous!"

Mom straightened. "I am not. I'm just disappointed in Phil's lack of taste."

"Did they come together?"

"Yes," she answered with a tinge of sadness in her voice.

"Mom, he can't wait around for you for ever. There's only so many times you can turn a man down before he turns to someone else."

"I could give you the same advice," she said, snorted, then stormed off.

I was left to hold up the wall alone and watch as the mayor was introduced. Mr and Mrs Spellman approached the podium, with Justin following closely. His blond hair was getting a little long in front, and he brushed it out of his eyes. I remembered running my hands through that hair, how soft it was, how it smelled like salt when he'd return to our beach blanket after a swim.

Mrs Spellman kissed her husband. Justin shook his hand. Then they both took their seats. As the mayor began to speak, Justin's eyes roamed over the crowd. He found me and I knew he wasn't listening to a word his father was saying.

I chugged the rest of my water and escaped to the ladies' room.

I leaned over the sink and concentrated on breathing. In

and out. *Don't think about him*. Breathe in. Breathe out.

The door opened, and I hoped it wasn't my mother.

Worse. It was Tiffany.

"Well, looky here," she said. "You're missing the big speech."

"I'm not in the mood, Tiffany."

She stood still, glaring at me in the mirror.

I whipped around. "What?"

"Why don't you have any girlfriends, Clare?"

"I . . . I have friends," I stammered.

"Your brother and Nate Garrick don't count. Friends. That. Are. Girls. How come you don't have any?"

Before I could answer, she stepped closer. "I'll tell you why," she said, pointing her finger at me. "Because you're a stuck-up bitch who thinks you're better than everyone else."

"That's not true. This is a small town, and in case you didn't realize it, people aren't exactly friendly to me. . ."

"Oh, please. You don't even try. You latch on to your brother, your brother's friends, your brother's job, your brother's life. You've got nothing that's your own. You used to piss me off, but now I feel sorry for you."

She turned and headed for the nearest stall. Before closing the door she added, "Clare Fern, you're the loneliest person I've ever met."

SIXTEEN

My lack of girlfriends was not breaking news. And, yes, it bothered me, but I never dwelled on it. There was nothing I could do to change it, so why waste the energy? I didn't need girlfriends. I had myself. I had Perry. I had Nate. I had books and music and the ocean to swim in. I had my future, a blank slate, to look forward to. I'd make friends in college where no one knew who I was. Those were the facts I clung to in my lonely moments, and I never got too depressed over it.

But for some reason, being called out on my friendless state by Tiffany Desposito rankled me. It was one thing for *me* to know I had no friends. It was another thing entirely for other people to know. To talk about it. To laugh behind my back at it. Tiffany and her crew were the main reason no one would be friends with me anyway. She'd made it clear that anyone who associated with me would get the same treatment I got. And no one at Eastport High wanted that.

I felt lonely. And mad. Normally, when feelings like these rose up, I'd talk to Perry. But that wasn't exactly a good option right now.

I was still fuming from my encounter with Tiffany when I walked in the door at Yummy's a while later. I had to get out of the stuffy event and knew Yummy's would be safe with that witch working the banquet. So I'd called a cab and left the drama behind.

I selected a stool that had no one on either side and ordered a hot fudge sundae. My plan was to sit there and eat until I forgot all about my awful day. What it felt like to see a dead body. My annoyance with Mom. Perry tearing down the posters and making himself look even more guilty. Tiffany's words that only hurt because they were true. The investigation that wasn't getting anywhere. And mostly, I wanted to forget the way I felt when I'd seen Justin at the banquet. I wished I could say a magic word and make all my feelings for him disappear.

Maybe I'd get a lobotomy.

For now, I'd eat.

"What's your excuse?"

Apparently, there would be no peace for me at

Yummy's, either. I swivelled around to face Gabriel, standing behind me, holding a drink in his hand.

"My excuse for what?" I said.

"For looking at that bowl of ice cream like it was your last friend on Earth. I know what my excuse is for being here alone."

"And what's that?" I asked.

"My father got chewed out by the mayor today for not making any headway on the investigation. It's his first case since we came here and not only has he not solved it, but the body count doubled." He took a long swig from his straw. "Your turn."

"I'm hiding from everyone I know."

"Bad time at the banquet?"

"How'd you know I was there?"

His eyes swept down the length of my legs. "The girls don't usually dress like that for a night at Yummy's."

I'd forgotten about my attire. I tugged at the hem of my dress and pulled it down my thighs a bit. "So what are you doing here?"

"Dad's working around the clock, so I'm not exactly getting home-cooked meals. I just placed my order down at the end of the bar when I saw you come in. Mind if I stay?" He motioned his hand towards the empty stool beside me. "We don't have to talk about the case."

I took a bite of ice cream and considered it. "Maybe thinking about the case will help me stop thinking about . . . other stuff."

Gabriel sat and studied my face for a few moments. "Justin Spellman messed you up good, didn't he?"

I glared at him.

"Sorry. Back to the case."

"Anything on Billy?" I asked.

"Not yet. They're going to compare the bullet to the one from the first victim to see if it's a match. But that's all they have right now."

"Whatever happened with Joel Martelli and the stolen car?" I asked.

"Turns out he took it from some girl back in Boston, someone else he was cheating on the victim with. She refused to press charges and we had nothing to hold him with, so he's gone." He shook his head. "The victim really knew how to pick 'em, huh?"

"Why do you do that?" I asked.

"Do what?"

"You always call her 'the victim'. She had a name, you know. Victoria. I've never heard you once say her name. Why is that?"

His face turned bright red and he turned away from me. What was up with that? Was he embarrassed that I called him out on using too much cop-speak? Or was he angry?

"So what about you?" he snapped. "Have you picked up anything else?"

He used his fingers to make quotes as he said "picked up". That riled me.

"Are you mocking me?"

"No. Why so defensive? Do you have reason to be?"

"I have no reason to be defensive. I'm the only one who's got anywhere with this case. I'm the one who found the hole in the ceiling at the crime scene. I'm the one who got Joni to talk. I'm the one who found Billy's note."

Gabriel's lips tightened. "And none of those things had anything to do with supposed psychic ability. You're smart and you used common sense. That's all."

I let my spoon fall loudly on to the counter. I couldn't believe he was acting like such an ass. After everything, he still thought I was a fake. I wanted to cry. I wanted to slap him.

Instead, I walked out.

The car park was pretty empty for that time at night. The rain from the morning was coming back. A slow drizzle dripped on to my skin. It didn't feel that bad, considering how humid it was outside, but waiting for a cab was going to suck. I sure as hell wasn't going back inside, though.

"Clare!"

I spun around. "Leave me alone, Gabriel."

"I'm sorry."

"Go back inside."

"Please, just listen." He held my shoulders, forcing me to face him. A drop of rain trailed down his cheek. His eyes were pleading, almost tortured. "I'm a jerk."

I nodded slowly. "Go on. . ."

"I don't know why I say these things. I mean, I do know why. Because I don't agree with what your family does for a living. But I hate that I keep hurting you because of it. You're a good person and I like you." He paused and added, "More than I should."

I silently reminded myself to breathe.

"I'm sorry I say these things. It's . . . my past. . ."

I thought he was going to explain more, but instead he kissed me. Full on kissed me. I'd never been kissed by anyone but Justin. I was lucky he was holding my shoulders, because my knees weakened and I was pretty sure I couldn't feel my legs. He tentatively moved his hands down to the small of my back. My mouth opened under his, deepening the kiss. He moaned and pulled me tighter against his body.

And then a car horn honked.

I pulled back and looked. My mom pulled up next to us in her Prius, here to destroy my moment, probably to get revenge on me for abandoning her at the banquet.

She rolled down the window and yelled, "Need a ride or are you already getting one?"

I groaned, but going with Mom was the smart thing to do. Staying here would lead to more kissing and I didn't know if I wanted that. Gabriel was gorgeous and smouldering and all those wonderful things, but he also seemed to hate who I was.

"See you later," I said to him and slid into the passenger seat.

Mom raised one eyebrow and gave a little whistle.

I elbowed her in the side.

Despite the slight stress headache I woke up with the next morning, I still had a little smile on my face. I'd been surprised by both Gabriel's kiss and my intense physical reaction to it. My emotions, however, were all over the place. Working on this case gave me a thrill like I'd never had before. And, despite how hot and cold Gabriel ran and how confusing my own feelings for him were, I had to admit I was enjoying being close to him. Last night's kiss told me he felt the same.

I shuffled into the bathroom, shook two Tylenol from the bottle, and downed them with a full glass of water. I'd feel better by the time I was out of the shower.

A half hour later, I was dressed in tan shorts and a green V-neck tee. I put on pale pink lipstick and scrunched some anti-frizz stuff into my crazy hair. I'd let my damp curls air dry and they'd look better soon enough. Humidity did terrible things to me. I'd be much prettier if I lived in the desert.

I hoped Gabriel had work for me today. I couldn't wait to see him again. I wondered if we'd talk about the kiss or pretend it never happened. He was probably as mixed up as I was, but the one thing I knew for sure was that I wanted to be near him. I checked my phone, but had no messages. With a sudden hankering for an unhealthy breakfast, I decided to walk to the convenience store for a doughnut.

I grabbed my bag but couldn't find my house keys. I always toss them on the kitchen counter when I come in. I vaguely remembered doing that last night after Mom and I got home. But I was still in a fog from Gabriel's unexpected kiss, so maybe I put them somewhere else by mistake.

The doorbell rang, so I had to temporarily abandon the search. Hoping it was Gabriel, I primped myself quickly and opened the door. The person I least expected stood on the other side.

"My name is Olga Maslov," she said, with a strong Russian accent.

"I know who you are." I jutted my chin out. "What can I do for you?"

She tilted her head to the side, her eyes closed. "You will find your keys on the floor."

My mouth opened. "How did you..."

Her eyes opened and snapped to attention. "That is not the reason I am here. I am here to warn you." Her eyes peered over my shoulder, presumably to see if I was alone.

"About what?"

"You are in danger."

"OK. Can you be more specific?"

"Not at this time. The ... um ... how do you say ... specific is unclear. But you are in grave danger."

Suddenly, the proverbial light bulb lit up in my head. "Ah. Let me guess, you want me to leave town to protect myself?"

She smiled broadly. "Yes, that would be wise."

"And maybe my brother and mother, too? Leaving you as the only game in town during peak season."

Maslov frowned and shook her head. "No. I do not care

about the business things. This warning is not to stop the competition. I'm telling you this for your own good."

"Sure, lady." I started closing the door but she held it open with her surprisingly strong arm.

"You must believe me," she whispered.

With one last disappointed shake of her head, Maslov walked off. I watched her for a moment, then closed the door. She was a crazy woman. She wanted to scare us off so she could have all the summer business. That was all. Plus, she was a fraud.

I walked over to the counter where I remembered chucking my keys. Then I wondered if maybe I had tossed too hard. I got down on my hands and knees and saw the silver glinting at me from under the fridge. I had flung them too hard and they'd bounced off and slid.

On to the floor.

SEVENTEEN

I put Maslov's dire warning and her correct guess about my keys out of my mind and walked to the store. The doughnut lasted only the first thirty seconds of my walk home. That poor thing never stood a chance. When I came back, I found Mom in the kitchen putting a bagel in the toaster.

"Want one?" she asked. "I got plenty."

"Nah. Just had a doughnut."

Mom raised one eyebrow. I knew what was coming. She grinned and said, "So..."

"Don't go there, Mom."

She moved her hips back and forth and sang, "Clare and Gabriel, up in a tree, k-i-s-s-i-n-g. First comes—"

"First comes a hissy fit if you don't stop," I interrupted.

"Fine, fine."

Her bagel popped out of the toaster and she covered it liberally with peanut butter.

"Where's Perry?" I asked.

"I heard the shower running a little while ago, so he should be joining us soon."

I thought about the last time I'd seen my brother, when I found the flyer with the picture of Victoria in his room. His state of mind had not been good. I was worried. Nate was worried. Then I realized . . . Mom would be worried, too, if she happened to be reading my thoughts right now. I hurried out of the kitchen, calling over my shoulder, "I'm going to sit on the porch!"

Unfortunately, Mom followed me.

I sat on an old wicker chair and focused on the nice warm weather, the cars going by, the girl walking her dog. Anything that would keep my mind off Perry, while Mom stood staring at me, munching her bagel.

"You really think I don't already know?" she said.

Damn it. "You picked it up from me?"

"No, you've hidden it quite well until now. Mr Mopey has been trying to hide upstairs, but anytime he's around it's all he's thinking about."

"Why haven't you said anything?"

"I didn't know you knew and, well, I didn't quite know what to do about it."

"What do you think he should do?" I asked.

"I think he should go to the police."

"Why? He'll become the top suspect!"

"But if he hides it from the police and they find out some other way, it'll make him look more guilty than if he had voluntarily shared the information."

"But the police might never find out," I said.

"Aren't you required to tell them? You *are* working for them now."

"Unofficially. Plus, I can help them without sacrificing my own brother."

"If they find out, you could be charged yourself."

"I don't care, Mom."

She put her plate down on the porch railing and took me by the shoulders. "I don't want both my kids in jail because of this. Honesty is best."

"Nobody's going to jail," I said, though I wasn't really sure about that.

The screeching of tyres made us both turn towards the road. Gabriel's Jeep pulled into the driveway. My heart fluttered a bit. *Maybe it's not business,* I thought. *Maybe he wants to see me again, continue last night's interrupted kiss.*

A police car pulled in behind him.

"What's going on?" Mom asked.

I didn't know. Gabriel got out of his car with a dark look on his face. He certainly wasn't here to try to kiss me again. And if he had work for me, he wouldn't have brought backup.

He climbed the front stairs and came right to me. "I'm sorry."

I shook my head in confusion. "For what?"

The screen door opened behind us, and Perry poked his head out. "What's happening?"

Gabriel moved aside as his father ascended the stairs and said, "Periwinkle Fern, you need to come with us."

EIGHTEEN

I stepped in front of my brother and put my hand on Detective Toscano's chest, pushing him back a bit. "Are you arresting him?" My voice had a panicked screech to it that I didn't bother trying to hold back.

He moved around me and spoke to Perry. "We are requesting that you come to the station and answer questions about your relationship with Victoria Happel."

Someone *had* seen him that night.

Someone told.

Gabriel wouldn't look me in the eye. His voice low, he said, "The results are in. The same gun was used to kill Victoria and Billy."

"But that has nothing to do with Perry," I said petulantly.

"Actually," Detective Toscano held up a sheet of paper, "we have a warrant here to search the house for that gun."

"Go right ahead," I said, holding my arms open wide. "Search all you want. You won't find a murder weapon here."

Perry's eyes widened and he shook his head slightly. Was he telling me no? Telling me not to let them in? I cocked my head to the side in confusion and everyone turned to look at Perry. He immediately cast his eyes down.

"We'll be respectful of your belongings as we execute the search warrant," Detective Toscano said, more to my mother than me since I was staring at Perry trying to figure out what that panicked look had been for.

Three more officers had come up behind us during all of this. One of them had handcuffs dangling from his right hand.

"Those won't be necessary," Perry said. "I'll come to the station voluntarily."

I watched helplessly as my brother was led to a police car and put in the back seat. My brother, who was always calm, always collected. The constant voice of reason in the family. The only one who could keep my mom's head from exploding when she got stressed. The only one who could make me feel safe when bullies picked on me for being a freak. The only one who could make me laugh after I broke up with Justin and felt my life crumbling around me.

He was more than my brother. He was my best friend.

Perry turned around and gazed out of the rear window as the cruiser pulled away. I held one hand up, palm out, until the car was out of sight. Then I sank down on to the porch. I fought off the urge to cry. I had to stay strong. I had to hold it together for Mom and Perry.

Mom's worried voice fluttered around behind me as she led the officers into the house for the search. I tried to drown out those sounds by focusing on how this could have happened.

If someone had seen Perry with Victoria that night, why wait so long to come forward as a witness? It didn't make any sense. It's not like someone could have just found out about it now. . .

I faltered as a thought clicked in my brain like a puzzle piece. But it couldn't be. There was no way in hell. . .

I stood up and broke into a run.

The newspaper offices were quaint and located in Eastport centre, between the town hall and the post office. THE EASTPORT TIMES was painted on the large glass storefront window, though the *P* was a little chipped at the bottom and needed to be touched up. A small space for a small-time paper.

I paused for a moment at the door, to wipe the sweat off

my brow and catch my breath. Then I walked in like I belonged there and headed straight to Nate's desk. His head was partially obscured by a giant computer monitor. He was hunched over, scribbling furiously on a notepad.

He glanced up at the sound of my stomping feet headed his way. "Hey, Clare, what's up?"

I tried to sneak a peek at his notepad. "What are you working on?"

"Putting together a story on our esteemed new detective and his not so esteemed past."

I rolled my eyes. "Still gnawing on that same bone, huh?"

The large, open room was filled with noise, from clicking keyboards to loud phone conversations.

Nate tapped his pen on the desk. "Do you know what Gabriel's tattoo says?"

"No, why?"

"Just curious. Trying to fill in the gaps here."

"I can try to find out."

Nate started to nod, then stopped. "No, don't. I don't want to put you in danger."

"What about Perry?"

"What about him?"

"You didn't mind putting him in danger."

Nate paused, waiting for the punch line, then realized I was serious. "Clare, I'm not following you."

"He was just brought down to the station," I said, trying to control the anger in my voice. "Someone told the police that he was with Victoria Happel the night she was killed. And it's interesting to me because Perry and I haven't told anyone this whole time. And then last night I told you and this morning Perry's taken away."

Nate's mouth opened in shock, then his face crumbled and his eyes took on a desperate look. I immediately knew what I should never have questioned. Nate was loyal.

"I didn't tell anyone," he pleaded. "You have to know that I would never do that."

I sat down hard on a swivel chair from a neighbouring cubicle and rolled it next to his. "I know. I'm sorry. I never should have thought it, even for one second. But the timing. . ."

"It could have been any number of people from the restaurant," Nate said. "Or the motel."

"But why now? Why wait a week to tip off the police?"

"Maybe they weren't paying attention to the news. Maybe they didn't put two and two together until now. Maybe they were thinking Perry Fern couldn't have done it and that the police would find the real killer, but then when nothing happened they figured they had to be honest?" Nate shrugged. "I really have no idea."

I leaned forward and put my face in my hands. "Until

this point, the police had no leads. Billy Rawlinson obviously witnessed it, but chose to try to make some side money rather than go to the cops, and now he's dead, too. All they have is the person who was last with the victim and that's Perry."

"I still don't think that's enough," Nate said. "They'll need more."

"Speaking of, they're ransacking the house right now. I'd better get back to Mom and try to keep her together."

Nate looked at me closely. I felt the sweat dripping down my neck.

"Did you run here?" he asked.

I shrugged. "I had to talk to you. I had to know."

He nodded. "Let me drive you back. I'm due for a break anyhow."

Nate sped back to the house and dropped me off in the street because the cops were blocking the driveway. I saw them loading Perry's computer into the back of a squad car. As I approached, an officer nodded at me. "We're done."

I found Mom in the living room curled up tight on the couch. With her face hidden and her long curly locks shaking as she sobbed, she looked like a lost little girl. I gently sat beside her and rubbed her back, something that would normally have been Perry's job.

"It's going to be OK," I whispered.

She looked up at me, mascara running down her cheeks. "But what if it's not? What if they arrest him?"

"I don't think they'll have enough," I said. "Sure he was with her, but they have no evidence that he killed her."

"They took . . . stuff from the house."

"Yeah, sure, but they won't find what they need. No murder weapon."

I fetched her a tissue. She sat up straight and wiped her face. "Thanks, sweetheart."

The phone rang and I grabbed it.

"Clare?"

The voice was familiar, but I couldn't immediately place it. "Yes?"

"This is Stephen Clayworth."

"Uh, hi. This is kind of a bad time."

"I know. That's why I'm calling. I heard they took Perry into custody. Did they arrest him?"

"Not yet, as far as I know. They're just questioning him."

"Do you have a lawyer?" he asked.

I hadn't even thought of that in all the chaos. "No, not yet."

"Come to my house and I'll set you up with our family's lawyer."

Great. The Clayworths' lawyer was probably the highest paid in the state. "Oh, I don't really think we could afford—"

"Don't worry about that part," Stephen interrupted. "Just get here and I'll help you out."

Could I have been any more wrong about him last year? I wanted to slap myself. "Thank you so much, Stephen. I'll be there soon."

"Was that Stephen Clayworth?" Mom asked as soon as I returned the phone to its cradle.

"Yeah. If we head to his house now, he'll set us up with his family's lawyer."

Her forehead creased. "Are you two..."

"No, not at all. We've mended fences. Turns out he's not that bad of a guy."

Mom grabbed her purse and car keys, and we sprinted outside. I skidded to a stop a few feet from the car. The front left tyre was flat.

"Huh," Mom said. "I hadn't even realized it was low before."

I knelt down to examine it.

"It wasn't low before," I said. "It's been slashed."

NINETEEN

"My tyre was fine this morning," Mom said.

"And no one would have slashed it while the police were here," I added.

We looked at each other. Whoever slashed the tyre had done it within the last ten minutes. I jogged down the street a bit, looking for anyone on the sidewalk.

A boy, about twelve years old, was riding his bike towards me. I held my hand out and stopped him. "Did you see anyone else on the street?" I asked him.

"Um, yeah, lots of people," he answered, with a "duh" tone of voice.

"Specifically, anyone maybe running away from this house? Someone slashed my mom's tyre."

He shrugged. "There was a chick with a beach bag and a big ugly hat, and she seemed in a hurry."

"Luke!" A girl with long blonde hair waved to him from down the street.

"Sorry. Gotta motor."

Ah, the pull of the blonde. It starts so young. Speaking of blonde, I knew who'd slashed the tyre. Tiffany. I didn't have time to deal with her now, though. I had to get help for Perry, but now we had no way to get to Stephen's house.

A shiny black car I recognized as Mr Spellman's pulled to the kerb. Justin leaned his head out of the window. "Get in!"

Not exactly a knight on a white horse, but I'd take it.

Mom slid into the passenger seat, I jumped in the back, and Justin sped off.

"I heard about Perry being taken in," he explained. "My father called a friend of his, a lawyer, and he's meeting us at the station."

"You don't have your licence yet," I said.

"But I can drive with my learner's permit as long as an adult is in the car." He smiled. "Hi, Mrs Fern."

Mom patted him on the shoulder. She'd always liked Justin and had made clear to me her feeling that he deserved a second chance. I sighed. Now that he had come to the family's rescue, she'd be on my case even more.

*

"I'm sorry. I really am," Gabriel whispered to me at the station.

"Your father is just doing his job." I wrung my hands as I babbled. "If Perry was with Victoria that night, he has to question him. I don't blame you. Soon, you'll see that Perry didn't do it. Your father will release him, and you and I can get back to . . . working on the case."

He turned away, as if he wasn't so sure about that. But neither was I.

I slumped into a hard plastic chair. I hated sitting there in the waiting area, knowing my brother was being held in a tiny room somewhere in the building, scared and unsure. I hoped they weren't battering him with questions. I hoped he was smart enough to refuse to answer until we got him a lawyer.

Anthony Toscano came into the room, and Gabriel immediately popped up and rushed to his father's side. Anthony was whispering in Gabriel's ear as I approached.

"Excuse me, Detective Toscano?"

He turned and looked down at me. I felt like a tiny little girl next to him. "Yes, Miss Fern?"

"May I speak with my brother for a moment? The lawyer should be here soon. I want to make sure he's OK."

A look came over his face. Was it pity? "Sure, follow me."

I nearly had to run down the hallway to keep up with his long strides. He was silent during our short walk, so I took in the surroundings. A flickering fluorescent light in the ceiling. A cigarette burn on the vinyl floor. The grey walls that begged for a paint job.

Detective Toscano stopped abruptly, and I nearly bumped into his back. "You've got two minutes," he said, and opened the door.

Perry jumped in his seat at the sound of the door slamming open, but his panic eased when he saw me. I tried to smile, but he'd know it was fake anyway. I didn't know if I was allowed to hug him or not. It all felt so surreal, like we were the victims of an elaborate prank.

I wish.

I sat in the chair opposite him and folded my hands on the table. "Are you all right?"

He shrugged.

"They treating you OK?"

"Yeah. They haven't done much. Gave me a drink."

"You weren't questioned?"

"I think they're waiting on a lawyer."

"Mr Spellman must have told them," I said. "The Spellmans' lawyer is going to represent you. He's on his way here. They'll probably start questioning you when he gets here."

He nodded, staring down at his hands. His face was a sickly shade of green. I figured there was a fifty-fifty chance he'd vomit all over the table.

"It's going to be fine, Perry."

"You don't know that," he whispered.

"You didn't do this, right?" I asked, trying to keep the quiver out of my voice.

"No." He looked me dead in the eyes. "I didn't."

I pushed any doubts I had away and focused on helping my brother. I grabbed his hands. "They can't charge you if you didn't do it."

"Sure they can. It happens all the time."

"Only in movies and mystery novels," I said, knowing that wasn't completely true.

Perry didn't reply, just stared down, his spirit broken. I strained to think of something else to say, but the words eluded me, so I squeezed his hands tighter. We sat there, holding hands in silence, until Detective Toscano returned and told me my time was up.

He led me back to the waiting area. Gabriel was gone. A dignified, grey-haired man in a suit was talking in low tones to my mother, who looked horrified.

"What is it?" I said, hurrying up to them.

The man looked at me quizzically.

Mom said, "This is my daughter, Clarity." Then

she turned to me, "This is Mr Nelson, Perry's lawyer."

"Nice to meet you," I said, though I really wanted to skip the pleasantries and find out what was going on.

"There's a problem," Mom said. "When they executed the search warrant they found something."

"The murder weapon? It must have been planted! There's no way—"

"No, not the weapon," Mr Nelson said. He stood stiffly and spoke in a soft yet authoritative voice. "They found the security tape from the restaurant car park. The one that shows your brother leaving with the victim the night she was killed."

The tape that was stolen. Stupid Perry! "He probably took it so they wouldn't see him with Victoria and think he did it," I said. "He *didn't* do it, though."

"An action like that adds to the pile of circumstantial evidence that he says did. Taking that tape and hiding it shows a purposeful attempt to cover something up." He sighed. "I wish he hadn't done that. It's going to make this much more difficult."

"I need to see that tape. The real killer might be on there."

"Clarity," he said, "according to the police, the real killer is already in custody."

*

The lawyer kept repeating that there was nothing we could do and told us to leave. He'd call when the police had reached a decision whether to arrest Perry or let him go home. It would most likely be several hours.

Mom went home, but I couldn't go back there. I imagined myself pacing the hall and listening to my mother's imminent breakdown. Instead, I headed to the one place that could calm my nerves. The beach.

I realized from the sun's position in the sky that it was the afternoon and I hadn't eaten lunch. But I wasn't the slightest bit hungry. I held my sandals and walked barefoot on the warm sand, avoiding areas dense with people. I didn't want to risk seeing anyone from school. Word about Perry was probably spreading like an STD.

I cut a path towards the water, intending to let the waves lap at my feet. But instead, I stopped. I came upon a sight that, days ago, would have filled me with butterflies. Gabriel was only a few feet away, in front of me, sitting on the sand. He had on cargo shorts. His shirt was off, tossed to the side. His back was tan and muscled. As he stared out at the sea, I wished I had my mother's gift so I could read his mind.

As if he could read mine, he turned around.

"Hey," he said, standing. He brushed the sand off his

shorts. His taut chest was a welcome sight, but even that couldn't make me smile.

Confused feelings rushed at me. My physical attraction to him was so strong, but my mind held back my heart. He didn't believe in me or my family. He scorned me for my gift, and he wouldn't even tell me why. Why did he care if I was psychic? Did that change the kind of person I was?

I could see the conflict on his face, too. He hated what my family did for a living. He probably believed my brother was a killer.

But he had feelings for me. I knew it. I saw it in his eyes.

He opened his arms. I ignored the part of me that wanted to push him away. I needed someone right now. I needed support. And he was here, offering it. I rushed into him and wrapped my arms around him, letting his heat envelop me. He hugged me, tight and warm.

"I'm so worried about him," I said.

"I understand," he whispered, as he ran his hands through my hair.

"I love Perry more than anything in the world."

"I know," Gabriel said. "I know what it's like."

His hands came to rest on my chin, turning my face up to look at him. He gazed into my eyes for a long moment.

A lump of frustration stuck in my throat. His touch was

tantalizing and I wished that I didn't enjoy it so much. Wished that I didn't want more from this guy who clearly disliked part of who I was.

I could see the struggle in his eyes. Stick to his convictions? Or give in to his feelings?

My heart pounded harder than the surf behind us.

Finally, he spoke. "I'm tired of trying to hate you."

Then he leaned in and kissed me.

I surrendered my head to my heart and let myself go. I was tired of fighting the attraction, worrying about my pride. I returned his kiss eagerly. I lost myself in the taste of his mouth and the feeling of his hands cupping my face. I was swept away in the moment, as wave after wave crashed on to the shore behind us.

I eventually had to break away to breathe. I pulled back to look at him, my hands trailing up his arms and on to his biceps. I turned my head to the side as he laid a trail of kisses down my neck.

Something caught my eye.

His tattoo.

I could see it a bit now. It was a word, written in cursive. Probably a name. Part of me didn't want to read it. If it was a girl, someone he had loved and left behind in New York, I'd feel insanely jealous, even though I had no right to. Curiosity got the better of me, though.

I tilted my head further. I silently prayed, *Please let it say Mom. Please say Mom. Please say Mom.*

It was a name, in flowery, feminine letters.

Not Mom.

Victoria.

TWENTY

Before I could scream, someone else did.

I broke away from Gabriel and stumbled back a few steps. He didn't notice my distress over his tattoo. His eyes were elsewhere.

A ways down the beach, a woman was screaming hysterically. A small crowd had gathered in the area, circling around something. Gabriel took off and I ran after him. As we got closer, the woman stopped screaming and fainted into a man's arms. The circle of people grew, amid gasps and exclamations.

I didn't want to see what they were looking at. It couldn't be anything good. My worst fear was that it was a baby dolphin, beached and dying. I couldn't watch that. I skidded to a stop in the sand, but Gabriel grabbed my hand and pulled me forward between two people in the crowd, until we saw what lay on the shore.

It wasn't a dolphin.

Worse. It was a person.

My mind screamed at myself to turn away, look away, run away, but my muscles wouldn't comply. I could only stare. It was a female, her face covered in seaweed. She wore jean shorts and a T-shirt. Where her skin showed, her body was discoloured and bloated.

I needed to know who she was. While everyone else stood and stared, I knelt on to the sand and reached forward to slide the seaweed off her face.

I'm sitting on the beach, staring at the black expanse of the ocean. It must be the middle of the night because it's dark and deserted. But I sense movement. I turn around and see a shadow. Someone's coming towards me.

"Hello," I call out.

Whoever it is doesn't answer, but speeds up, coming at me with determination. I'm suddenly scared. A trickle of sweat slips down my back.

My instincts kick in. I leap up and run for the boardwalk. I risk a glance over my shoulder. The shadow is charging after me. Getting closer. The stairs are too far away; I'll never make it. I dash under the boardwalk, hoping to become invisible in the darkness.

The shadow enters. I creep further down. It's like a sick game of hide-and-seek. My breathing is harsh and ragged.

It's too loud; it's going to give me away. I try to hold my breath, but I'm too terrified.

After a few moments, I glance left and right, but can't find the shadow. Did the person give up? I start to feel like it's over, and then arms grab me from behind, hands wrap around my neck. I can't breathe—

"Clare!"

I opened my eyes to find Gabriel dragging me backwards, away from the body. He dropped me on the sand and sank down beside me.

"Are you OK?"

"I saw it," I said. "I saw her death. She was strangled under the boardwalk. I couldn't see who did it."

I stopped and looked up at Gabriel. "Who is she?"

He shook his head. "Don't look."

I pushed myself up and, dizziness be damned, trudged back to the body. My eyes first went to the ragged, bitten fingernails. Then her long brown hair. Then her face. I immediately recognized her.

Joni. It was Joni. Victoria's best friend. The one I gave the reading to. The one I forced to give a statement to the police. The one who was terrified of Victoria's boyfriend, Joel. And now she was dead.

Suddenly, the smell hit me like a punch. I only made it a few steps away before my stomach contents poured on to the sand. Gabriel came to my side and rubbed my back with one hand, while holding my hair back with the other, until I regained my composure.

"Joel must have killed her," I said between deep breaths. "No one else here even knew Joni. She wasn't even here when Victoria was here."

"Joel is gone, though," Gabriel said. "When the girl from Boston wouldn't press charges for the stolen car, they let him go."

"That doesn't mean he didn't kill her."

"But he wasn't here when she would have died."

"How do you know? Maybe he didn't leave town. Or maybe he did and came back." I raised my voice to match my rising frustration. "You and your father have your sights set on Perry and you won't even consider anyone else, even when the evidence points that way!"

"The evidence points towards your brother!" Gabriel yelled back.

I couldn't believe he was being so shortsighted, not even considering Joel. Seething with fury, I clenched my fists. I stepped up to him, inches from his face. "I want you to listen carefully. There will be no us. Ever. I'm done working with you. Now, I'm working against you."

I stomped away and called over my shoulder, "Because someone has to find the real killer."

I ran home as fast as I could. I should have been there the whole time anyway. Mom was all alone in the house, waiting for the phone call, and I was making out with the enemy on the beach. I was as angry with myself for that kiss as I was with Gabriel for his stubbornness. And on top of it all, his tattoo revealed he had a secret of his own. I couldn't trust him. I was on my own now.

I sprinted up the porch stairs and into the house. "Mom?"

"In here."

I burst into the kitchen. "Any calls?"

"Not yet," she said, placing a fizzy drink can on the table. Nate was sitting there, ripping a napkin into a thousand pieces, worry written all over his face.

"Hey," I said, taking a seat beside him.

Mom fluttered around the kitchen like a trapped bird. She seemed to be doing anything to keep herself busy.

"I came by to keep you two company," Nate said. "And maybe because I needed the company, too." He tried to smile, but it quickly faltered. "I'm worried, Clare."

"I am, too. But it's going to be OK," I said, straightening in my seat and trying to fill my voice with hope.

Mom turned the water off in the sink. "Has something happened?"

I took a deep breath. "Joni's dead. Her body's on the beach; the police are probably there now."

Mom gasped and covered her mouth.

"That's terrible," Nate said. "Did she drown?"

"No. She was strangled and dumped in the water. By whoever killed Victoria and Billy, I'm sure. I think, now more than ever, this points to Joel, Victoria's boyfriend."

Mom nodded, her eyes staring out of the window. "I hope the police see it that way."

Mom went out to the porch for some fresh air, instructing us to sit by the phone.

"There's something else, too," I whispered to Nate. "I saw Gabriel's tattoo."

He gestured dismissively. "I don't care about that story any more. I'll work on it when this is over."

"Victoria," I said.

"What about her?"

"The tattoo. It says 'Victoria'."

Nate's eyes narrowed.

"It could be a coincidence," I said. "There are thousands of Victorias out there."

"But only so many killers," he said softly.

"What does that mean?"

"I made gains on the story. I found out why the Toscanos left New York City. Anthony didn't quit the NYPD, he was fired."

"For what?"

"He killed someone."

My mind churned with shock and confusion. "He would be in jail if that were true."

"It was in the line of duty so no criminal charges were filed. However, the use of deadly force was ruled unjustified, and he lost his job. The whole case is really shady. There was something personal between him and the guy he killed."

"That's awful," I said. "But what does that have to do with what's going on now?"

"A killer's a killer. He's used his badge as a way to murder someone and get away with it before. What if he did it again?"

I thought about Billy's crime scene and how someone had been watching us in the woods. It could have been Detective Toscano. I thought about how Gabriel refused to say Victoria's name, insisting on referring to her as "the victim", despite having that same name tattooed on his arm. Was it possible that…

No. No way.

"You can't jump to that conclusion without knowing more details," I said, both to Nate and myself.

"Why not?" Nate snapped. "They were happy to jump to conclusions about Perry."

He had a point. "I do know something that might help us," I said. "I asked Detective Toscano if I could see the security tape and he refused. If that tape shows him or Gabriel at the restaurant that night, then maybe your theory is right."

Nate perked up. "You have to get that tape. It could be our only chance to free Perry."

"But how? I can't just break into the police station and steal it."

"There is one way," Nate said, rubbing his chin. "Justin. He'd do anything for you and his father could easily get the tape."

"You want me to *use* Justin?"

"*Use* is a terrible word. He'd probably enjoy the attention. Bat your eyes, swish your hair, whatever it is that girls do to get guys to stumble over themselves."

I took a deep breath. I'd do anything for my brother.

"OK," I said. "Whatever it takes."

I texted Justin, asking him if we could meet and talk. Lightning quick, he replied saying he'd meet me on the boardwalk. I expected him to say the beach, since that was our spot. But he must have heard about Joni by now. If there's one thing that will kill a romantic moment, it's a crime scene.

I rushed down to the boardwalk. Somehow, Justin had made it there before me.

He was waiting on a bench, his left leg bouncing up and down like it did when he was anxious. He wore khaki shorts and a white polo shirt that showed off the summer tan on his arms. He spotted me and stood with an apprehensive smile.

"Hey."

"Want to walk?" I asked.

"Whatever you want." He fell in line beside me and we walked slowly down the boardwalk. "I'm glad you texted me. We need to talk."

My eyebrows rose. I wasn't expecting him to have his own agenda. "What's up?"

"There's been another murder."

"I know," I said. "Joni. It's horrible."

The vision of her death tickled at my memory, and I pushed it away. I couldn't think about it. I needed to be strong right now, not have a breakdown.

"I think it's time for this to stop," Justin said.

I gave him a blank look. "What do you mean?"

"I don't want you involved in the investigation any more. At first, I thought it was a good idea. You could help us solve the case quickly, get the guy behind bars, and we'd move on. I never imagined for a second that you would be in danger. I would never have asked you to help. But now Billy's dead and Joni's dead. This person's unhinged. I don't want you working on this any more. I want you to just stay home until it's over."

This was exactly why I hadn't told anyone about the vision I'd had of someone watching me in the woods. I knew it would lead to this. Whether it was Perry, Justin, or Mom who found out, they'd all want me to stop. But I couldn't. I'd had my doubts about Perry before, but they were gone now. Seeing him at the police station, looking into his eyes, I knew. I never should have suspected him for a moment. He's my brother. I know him. He'd never touched a gun in his life; he wouldn't know what to do with one. Yeah, he could treat girls a little better, but he wasn't a killer. He just plain didn't have it in him. And now that Joni was dead, too, there wasn't a doubt in my mind that my brother was innocent. And the place in my heart that had once wavered was now filled with resolve.

I had to save him.

"I appreciate your concern, Justin, but I can't do that."

"Why not?"

"My brother could go to jail for the rest of his life and I know he didn't do it. The police aren't going to help him; they're convinced he's guilty. All Perry has is me. I'm not going to quit on him now."

Justin stuffed his hands in his pockets and sighed. "I know where you're coming from. But if anything happens to you..."

"It won't."

"You can't guarantee that."

"I can't stop. Perry needs me."

Justin nodded, giving in. "I know there's no way Perry did this."

I stopped walking and looked up at him. The sun's rays made his hair look golden. His blue eyes were deep and soulful. He looked like a prince from a fairy tale. My mind flitted to where the fairy tale went wrong, but I forced it back to the moment at hand.

Gabriel assumed Perry's guilt. Justin assumed his innocence. Justin had come to my family's rescue, driving Mom and me to the station, arranging for a lawyer. He was always there for me.

I reached up and put my hand on his cheek.

Then I kissed him.

That wasn't part of the plan. I had no intentions of locking lips with my ex, tape or no tape, but I lost myself in the moment and went with it. His kiss was tentative, light. Like our first kiss on the beach, so long ago. I remembered his mouth, his taste, his kissing style.

Kissing Gabriel was like an exotic vacation.

Kissing Justin was like coming home again.

I wanted this.

Until he pushed me away.

"What do you want?" he asked with his arm out, holding me at a distance.

I blinked rapidly, not understanding what happened. "Excuse me?"

"This is a dream come true, but I know it isn't real. You want something. Tell me what it is. You know I'll do it."

I hesitated, full of confusion. I hadn't kissed him to get the tape. I'd kissed him because I wanted to. I'd been overcome. I was able to temporarily push Tiffany out of my thoughts and give in to my feelings.

But I didn't want him to know that. My guard had slipped for one moment, that was all. I didn't want to fill him with false hope.

"I want to see the tape," I said, instead.

He turned away from me and leaned on the railing of the boardwalk. I watched his back. He shuddered once, then straightened and turned back to me.

I'd hurt him. Badly this time. I felt a pang of regret.

"The security tape from the restaurant?" he asked. "The one they found in your house? Why do you want that? Even if you destroyed it, that wouldn't help Perry."

"I don't want to destroy it or steal it. I want to watch it. Once."

He thought for a moment. "You think someone else might be on there. The real killer."

I nodded.

"How will you know, though? You could watch people go in and out of there all night and not recognize the killer."

"Or I could see Victoria's boyfriend, Joel, on there and place him at the scene. Or . . . someone else." I didn't want to share Nate's theory about the Toscanos being killers. I also didn't want Justin to know I'd seen Gabriel's tattoo. And I couldn't explain to myself why.

"I don't know," he said.

"This could be the key to everything." I put my hand on his arm, an old habit, and looked into his eyes. "We could break the case wide open. That's what you came to me for days ago. That's what you want the most, right?"

"No." He gently pulled his arm out from under my touch. "Honestly, what I want the most is to go back in time and change that night with Tiffany."

"Isn't that a little overdramatic, Justin?"

His face was tight. "I hurt you. I love you and I hurt you. I see the pain in your eyes even now. I see it every time you look at me." His voice broke. "Call me overdramatic, call me anything you want, but it's the truth."

This was exactly what I'd wanted the past few months. I'd wanted to hurt him, to watch his face twist in agony. To get him back for what he'd done. But I wasn't enjoying it. I realized with a rush of emotion that I didn't want Justin to be in pain.

Out of nowhere, it washed over me. The months of despising him, wanting to hurt him, not caring how many times he apologized. It washed away, and I felt a new feeling for the first time.

I reached out tentatively and put my hand on his.

"I forgive you," I said.

He looked up at me with hope in his eyes.

"I can't be with you," I said quickly. "But I forgive you. I believe that you wish you could go back and fix things. And that you never meant to hurt me."

He blinked quickly. His mouth opened, but no words came out.

"I'm not saying this just to get the tape," I added. It was true. Sure, at first I'd planned to use him, to manipulate his feelings for me to get what I wanted. But then all these feelings I'd buried had started to surface.

All these months I'd tried to hurt him with my words and my absence. I'd thought that hurting him would heal me. I never realized that what I needed to do to fix myself was to forgive him. He'd been punished enough. I might never be able to be his girlfriend again, but I could be his friend.

"I mean it," I said.

"I know you do," he said quietly and squeezed my hand.

TWENTY-ONE

My nerves prevented me from standing still for even a single moment, so I paced back and forth in the mayor's office. I felt good about forgiving Justin the day before on the boardwalk. It felt right and settled. But then I also felt guilty for feeling good about something while I still didn't have the answers I needed about Victoria's death.

Justin had been gone a long time. He should have been back by now. I started to worry. He'd said he buttered his father up over dinner last night and Mr Spellman had agreed to let us watch the tape. But what if he couldn't *get* the tape? What if this was another dead end? What if—

The door slammed open and Justin burst in, quickly closing and locking the door behind him. He held up a videocassette in his hands and waggled his eyebrows.

"Oh, thank you!" I rushed up to him, instinctively going for a hug, then held back.

This was all new to me. At first he was my boyfriend. Then my enemy. And now. . .? I didn't quite know how to act and didn't have the time to figure it out.

Thankfully, Justin didn't make the moment any more uncomfortable. He pulled a second chair over to the little A/V setup he'd put together, and pushed the tape into the VCR.

"Remember these things?" I said.

Justin was nervous. He looked around the office one last time and spoke, almost to himself. "OK, the door's locked. My dad's coming back in thirty minutes to get the tape and bring it back downstairs to the station. Ready?"

"Ready."

I pressed play. The tape was grainy but viewable and showed the front door of Yummy's. The security camera gave a bird's-eye view of who walked in and out. I held my finger on the fast-forward button until a person came into view, then I'd pause, slo-mo, then fast-forward again until the next customer. After a while, we found our first person of interest.

"There she is," I said, watching Victoria walk into Yummy's alone. She wore a revealing tank top and skinny jeans, her hips swaying with each step.

"Completely unaware that she's going to die," Justin said sadly.

An older couple came in after her. Then a gaggle of girls I knew from high school. Then a few seniors who had graduated came in together, including Stephen Clayworth. Tiffany came out for a smoke break. I bit my tongue and didn't say anything to Justin. That was a big step for me.

A ton of people I didn't recognize milled in and out, which wasn't surprising. It had been the biggest tourist weekend of the year.

"Isn't that. . ." Justin squinted at the screen.

"Gabriel Toscano," I said, mixed feelings making my voice tremble. Was Nate right about him? I didn't want to believe it.

My instinct couldn't be that off base, could it? I'd been attracted to, kissed, wanted ... a killer? I'd worked alongside him for days. It couldn't be. But her name was tattooed on his arm and here he was at Yummy's the night of the murder.

Something he'd never bothered to tell me before.

His father was running the investigation and getting nowhere. The same father who had killed someone back in New York. Maybe Gabriel didn't have something personal against psychics. Maybe the truth was he didn't want to work with me because he was scared I'd pick up on his guilt.

"Oh, here he comes back out," Justin said, snapping me out of my daze.

"What's that he's carrying?" I looked hard at the brown bag in Gabriel's arms.

"Takeaway," Justin said, dismissing it and fast-forwarding until a foursome of old men walked in.

Cecile Clayworth strolled in next, wearing a stunning emerald green, belted dress. What was she doing there? I figured she'd think Yummy's was beneath her. Perry went in next and not too long after that, Perry and Victoria came out together.

"Smooth operator," Justin said and whistled.

"Yeah, he's gifted," I mumbled.

Cecile came out, dragging a drunken Stephen. That explained her presence. She'd probably been called to take care of her son. I guessed the night at the boardwalk wasn't the first time he'd had one too many underage brews. The last thing Dallas Clayworth needed during his campaign was his golden boy being labelled as a boozebag.

"Well, that's it," Justin said, shutting off the tape minutes later. "That sucked. No Joel Martelli."

"We're not leaving this empty-handed, though," I said. "There is Gabriel Toscano."

Justin's forehead creased. "He went in for like a minute and came out with a bag of takeaway. I don't think that makes him a suspect."

"He was there, in the same place as the victim, and

never bothered to mention that while I've worked with him on the case for almost a week."

"So?"

I couldn't believe Justin was defending him. I had to tell him. "And he also has a tattoo on his bicep."

Justin's face changed. I knew he was going through all the scenarios in which I could have seen Gabriel with his shirt off. And he didn't like it.

"It says 'Victoria'," I finished.

Justin blinked rapidly. "I guess, um, that could be something, I don't know."

Someone knocked lightly on the door. I took the videotape out and hid it behind my back, just in case, as Justin unlocked the door. Thankfully it was only his father.

Mayor Spellman closed the door behind him and immediately turned to me. "Perry has been released."

I let out a huge breath and sank into the nearest chair.

He continued, "They have no weapon. They have no motive. They only have evidence that Perry and the victim were together, which Perry now admits, nothing else. Stealing the tape was a dumb move, but they can't hold him for only that."

"Thank God," Justin said.

"He has to stay in town," Mr Spellman continued. "And

they're not giving up. They're going to keep digging for more on him."

"That's OK," I said, rising from my seat. "They won't find more because he's innocent." I paused, looking at them. "I have you both to thank for this."

"Thank our lawyer, not us," Justin said.

I gave Mr Spellman back the tape and thanked him profusely again. He left to return the tape to the station downstairs.

"What's next?" Justin asked.

"Now I'm going to find out more information about what went on in Yummy's that night."

And I knew exactly who could help me.

I breathed in the moist, humid air as I walked home. The sun had almost completely set. I was starving and tired, but my mind raced. Things were happening so fast on so many different levels. My old feelings for Justin were rising to the surface again. My newer crush might actually be a killer, or the son of one. Perry had been released, but wasn't out of danger. I couldn't wait to get home and see him, but didn't know whether I should hug him or dope-slap him.

First I had one more thing to do. I pulled my mobile out of my pocket and dialled as I walked.

Stephen answered after a few rings.

"Hi, it's Clare Fern."

"Hey. What's up?"

"I wanted to call and tell you I'm so sorry."

A pause. "For what?"

"For not showing up today to meet your lawyer. Someone slashed my mom's tyre, if you can believe it. But I wanted to thank you for offering to help. Can I take you to dinner tomorrow night?"

"Um..." Stephen was obviously surprised by the offer, but he wasn't exactly saying no.

"I thought we were cool now, after our talk. Plus, it's not a date. Just one friend thanking another friend."

"Sure," he said. "That actually sounds great."

He seemed sincere, with a hint of excitement in his voice.

A small flame of guilt flickered inside me for lying to him and using him, but my need for answers quickly doused it.

TWENTY-TWO

The Fern family calendar was blank the next day. A rare event for July, but things add up. It was a Monday and the Fourth of July peak week was done. And, you know, the whole "a murderer lives there" thing isn't good for business.

Mom was handling it by cleaning. She was happy to have Perry home again, but our worries weren't over. To Mom, this called for obsessive, floor-to-ceiling scrubbing.

There was nothing I could do until my dinner with Stephen, so I spent the day with Perry, uselessly trying to lift his spirits. As annoying as man-whore Perry was, I wanted that old Perry back. He was better than depressed Perry. I'd rather roll my eyes at his constant conquests than sit in the living room beside him, wondering about his state of mental health.

"Come on," I said grabbing his arm. "We're going out."

I tried to pull him up off the couch, but he was dead weight.

"No," he moaned.

"It's a beautiful sunny day."

"I can't." He covered his face with a pillow.

"What are you, a vampire?"

"People will stare at me. They'll whisper," his muffled voice muttered.

"Perry, people always stare and whisper at us."

"Not like this."

I stomped my foot. Perry peeked one eye out from under the pillow.

"Yeah, I stomped. I'm your little sister and I want you to buy me some pizza. You *owe* me, Perry."

He moaned and groaned some more, but got up. And during our stroll to the boardwalk not one person pointed or stared. I nabbed us a bench with a great people-watching view and Perry bought us some slices from Monty's.

I took a bite and closed my eyes in a moment of pizza ecstasy.

Perry took a bite and all the cheese came with it, landing on his chin. He sighed and peeled it off. "Monty's pizza sucks. I know I owe you for trying to help clear my name, but you should've chosen ice cream."

"You don't just owe me for that." I wiped my mouth with a paper napkin.

"What else?" Perry asked, with his scarred eyebrow raised.

"I figured out why Tiffany Desposito targeted my boyfriend a few months ago. Turns out it was revenge, but she was taking it out on the wrong person."

"Oh, yeah?" His eyes slid down.

"A little birdie told me what happened between you two."

He grunted. "Nate."

I turned to face my brother. "You think it's all fun and games, hooking up with girls and ignoring them after. You act like there aren't any repercussions. But there are. You hurt her." I couldn't believe I was defending Tiffany of all people.

"You're right." He held his hands up in submission. "I thought it was just a meaningless party hook-up to her, too. It wasn't until she started acting psycho that I realized she'd hoped for something more." He shook his head slowly. "I never thought she'd direct her anger at you for what I did. That whole thing with Justin was low. I didn't know she was capable of that."

"Who knows what people are capable of," I said sadly.

"OK, now I feel super guilty." Perry nudged me a little

with his shoulder. "I'm going to buy you some ice cream, too."

I stayed on the bench and people-watched while Perry fetched us cones. Tourists strolled by, their shirts stained with ice cream, their skin sunburned, their faces happy. Townies always complained about the summer influx, the traffic and the crowds at the beach, but overall it was cool to grow up in a tourist town. The town's purpose was to make visitors happy and my family had a small part in that. I'm sure some people went home saying their Cape Cod vacation was so much fun and the best part was this psychic reading they had by a family of freaks. I smiled.

"Touch me, baby!"

I looked up and groaned. Cody and Trevor, two juniors from my school, friends of Tiffany and her crowd, walked by, laughing with delight.

"Yeah," Trevor yelled. "Touch my dick and tell me where it's been!"

"Easy," I called out. "It was in Cody's mom."

"Bitch," Cody muttered.

Thankfully they kept walking.

So much for me loving my town and my job. Ah, well. I closed my eyes and pressed my fingers to my temples.

"You know what I hate?"

Now what? I opened my eyes and found Madame

Maslov sitting beside me. She wore a white cotton dress, all the way down to her ankles, with lace up to her throat. Her feet were bare, crossed at the ankles. She looked over my shoulder at the ocean as she spoke.

"People always asking me for these numbers. I know not tomorrow's lottery numbers. I hate when they ask for this."

Was she trying to bond with me over the occupational hazards of being psychic?

"My gift does not work like that," she continued in her funny accent. "Just like your gift doesn't always work when you want it to." She looked at me then. Her eyes were dark and framed by laugh lines, which made them look kind. "Are you here to see me? You know what I spoke of before is true."

"No, I'm just here to get food. And I don't believe a word you said. You just want me and my family to leave town because we're your only competition."

"These things you say are not true," she said, tilting her head to the side. "The truth I know is that you are in danger. I tell you this before. I try to protect you but you're not good at the listening." She pointed at her ear for emphasis. "I try again." Maslov inched closer on the bench and looked at me determinedly. "Leave this place. Before it is too late."

I heard Perry's footsteps pounding on the boardwalk as he came up to the bench with an ice-cream cone in each hand.

"What's going on?" he asked.

"Nothing," I said. "Madame Maslov was just leaving."

I turned back to Maslov, but her attention was no longer on me. She was staring at Perry.

She stood and stepped up to him, cocking her head to the side. "You look so familiar to me. I met a man once who looked just like you, but older."

Perry immediately stiffened. My heart skipped a beat.

"Where?" I asked, trying to keep my voice casual.

Maslov waved her hand as if it wasn't worth mentioning. "Far, far away, in my homeland, in a deserted area."

Her watch beeped and she looked down at it. "I need to return to my business now."

She pulled a large ring of keys out of her purse and turned towards her shop, casting one last glance at me. A worried glance. Either she was a great actress or she really believed I was in danger.

"These are melting all over the place," Perry said. A puddle of sticky ice cream had formed at his feet.

"I'm not hungry any more."

Perry gave a tiny shrug and proceeded to chomp on both cones. "Wanna walk the beach?"

"No thanks. I'm going to head back."

I watched Perry descend the boardwalk stairs to the sand below. I was glad I got him out and about. Mission accomplished. I turned to start heading home, when someone caught my attention.

Cecile Clayworth was gliding towards Maslov's shop in a tight-fitting black dress and heels. Our eyes locked and she changed direction, charging towards me. I stopped and waited for her, curious what this could be about.

"I want to ask you something," Cecile said, getting right down to it.

"OK." I crossed my arms over my chest.

"You have a date with my son tonight."

I wouldn't exactly call it a date, but I nodded.

"I want you to cancel it."

I wasn't expecting that. Her tone rankled me. "I don't see why our dinner plans would be any of your business."

Cecile whipped off her oversized sunglasses. "You've caused my family a lot of trouble in the last few months. Your childlike need to tattle to the principal nearly took away my son's Ivy League spot and ended up costing my husband a lot of money."

I refused to let her rattle me. "You're putting the blame on the wrong person here," I replied. "If Stephen hadn't cheated on the test, none of the rest would have happened."

Cecile's expression remained cold. "You can think whatever eases your conscience, darling, but the truth of the matter is that you were the catalyst for that bit of trouble. Since then I have been civil and even cordial to you and your family. We have to share this town and despite everything you've done, my son has a soft spot for you. So, because of his wishes, I've been kind. But that will all end if you pursue my son. He deserves better than some gypsy-pretender."

I took a step into her personal space. "You're quite the snob for someone from such meagre beginnings."

"Excuse me?"

"It's no secret you're ex-trailer trash. You lucked out in the looks department, latched on to a rich dude and turned your life around. But don't pretend you're better than me."

"Stay away from my son."

She thrust her sunglasses back on and dismissed me like hired help. I wanted to knock her off her high heels, but assaulting Cecile Clayworth in the most public place in town wouldn't do much to help our floundering business. Instead, I marched home and got ready for my non-date.

TWENTY-THREE

Stephen showed up at my door wearing a blue button-down shirt and smart trousers. A bit overdressed for what I had planned, but Stephen was always overdressed. What surprised me were the roses he held out in his hand.

Hadn't I been clear that this was not a date? Granted, I hadn't been completely honest about my intentions to grill him for info. But I'd thought Stephen knew that this wasn't a romantic thing – just a thank-you dinner.

"Are you allergic?" he asked.

"Huh?"

"The roses," Stephen said. "You're frowning at them."

"Oh, I'm sorry. They're beautiful. I was just trying to remember where our vase is." I took them from his hand and did the obligatory sniff-and-smile.

"Thank you. I'll be right back." I quickly brought the flowers into the kitchen to ask Mom to put them in water.

She was on the phone. I could only hear one side of the conversation but it seemed like someone was insistently trying to set up a last-minute appointment. Mom explained that we were closed for the day, but the person must have been begging. Mom finally agreed to do a one-on-one. I felt bad, leaving her in the lurch, but I had to go.

Stephen walked me to his Lexus. "Where are we headed? The Captain's Bistro?"

"I was thinking Yummy's," I said.

"Okaaay," he said with slight disappointment. "If that's what you want."

It's not that I was craving Yummy's, not by any means. But if I wanted to jog Stephen's memory of the night Victoria was killed, Yummy's was the place to be.

"You've been here before," he said, after we were seated in a dimly lit corner booth.

"Yeah, I'm a regular. How'd you know?"

"You didn't look at the menu."

I smiled and pointed to my head. "I'm flipping through it right now."

He laughed. "I guess you do come here a lot. What's good?"

"My brother likes the burgers. I'm partial to the chicken fingers."

"How is your brother?"

Before I could answer, a waitress came over and took our order. After she left, I turned back to Stephen, who seemed genuinely concerned.

"Perry's not doing so well."

"But I heard the police set him free," Stephen said.

"They did, but he still remains their top suspect. They just didn't have enough to hold him at that time." I unexpectedly found myself fighting off the urge to cry. All day I'd been wearing a mask of confidence for my mother and Perry, and now that I was away from them and talking about it, I was close to breaking down.

"I'm so sorry," I said, dabbing at the wetness around my eyes with my napkin. "This summer has really sucked."

"I don't mind."

"How is your summer going?" I asked, changing the subject so I could regain my composure.

Stephen shrugged. "Not that great. With the campaign going on, it's just non-stop politics at the house. Going to fancy dinners with my parents. Being forced to schmooze. I've been under a lot of stress lately. My parents are out at another fundraiser tonight. I was supposed to go, but this is a nice change of pace."

I thought about telling him the terrible things his mother had said to me that afternoon, but decided to keep them to myself. He seemed to have enough parental problems at the moment.

"To be honest, I can't wait to go away to college next month. Get away from it all. My parents are very ... single-minded." He suddenly stopped. "I'm sorry. I shouldn't be talking about that."

"I don't mind. It's good to vent."

"No, that's personal, family stuff. And this is a nice night out. I'm sorry. I'm being a downer. Let's talk about something happy."

"Like how the town thinks my brother is a murderer?"

Stephen chuckled. "OK, OK. Your life isn't much better right now."

"You got that right."

The waitress came by with our food and Stephen quickly dug into his burger.

"I heard that you were working on the case with the police," he said. "Is that true?"

"It *was* true. But not any more."

He sighed in relief. "I'm so glad."

"Why?"

"You were putting yourself in danger doing that." He pointed at me with a French fry. "That one death has turned into three."

I appreciated everyone's concern for my well-being, but I didn't need another person telling me to stop. I took a deep breath, sensing the moment was right for my segue. I had to get the information I came for.

I cleared my throat. "Speaking of that night, I've been meaning to ask you. Did you see anything suspicious when you were here?"

"What do you mean?"

"You were here the night Victoria Happel and my brother left together. The night she was killed."

"I was? How do you know?" His eyes lit up. "Oh, wait, did you just pick that up in your head?"

"No, nothing psychic. It's on the security tape that my brother is on. You were, uh, drunk and your mother brought you home."

He rolled his eyes at himself. "I forgot that was the same night. How embarrassing."

"We all have our bad moments," I said. "Believe me, I've had mine. Remind me to tell you how I dumped a Coke over Tiffany Desposito's head right over there."

He smiled a little at that, then shook his head. "Sorry I can't help, but I didn't see anything weird that night."

"Did you see Victoria talking to anyone other than my brother?" *Like Anthony Toscano, the killer with a badge, or his son, Gabriel, the liar with the victim's name tattooed on his body?*

Stephen shook his head. "To be honest, I barely

remember that night. I spent the rest of it throwing up in the bathroom. I remember our housekeeper picking me up off the tile floor and helping me to bed."

"Ouch," I said, grinning.

"Yes, one of my mother's proudest moments, I'm sure."

I giggled.

He leaned forward, putting his arms on the table. "Now about this drink dumping. I have to hear this."

We spent the rest of dinner sharing school gossip and talking about different colleges. Surprisingly, I didn't have a bad time. Then the bill came and I realized I hadn't got any information that could help me clear Perry, and wasn't any closer to finding out if either of the Toscanos saw or spoke to Victoria that night.

Stephen paid the bill even though it was me who had asked him out. We strolled to his car and he opened the door for me.

"What do you want to do now?" he asked, after he settled in on the driver's side. "Do you need to get home?"

I had an idea. Stephen's alcohol-induced haze had made his memory of that night foggy.

But objects don't forget.

I swirled to face him. "Can we go to your house? You said your parents were out."

"Um..."

I could see him trying to figure this out, thinking he didn't picture me for that kind of girl.

"I've never seen the mansion," I added. "I wasn't invited to any of your parties in school." I smirked. "Not cool enough, I guess."

Stephen winced. "Sorry if I ever treated you badly."

"You didn't. You never teased me like the others. You just ignored me. But you can make up for it now," I said, grinning.

"OK then," he said, pulling out of the parking lot. "We're off for a tour of the Clayworth house."

Minutes later, Stephen parked in the circular driveway and walked me to the front door, which was flanked by two white pillars. I'd seen his house before from the street, but it was even more impressive up close. Stephen used his key, and I politely looked away as he punched in a code on the security system.

The entry hall had marble floors, a chandelier hanging from the ceiling, and a breathtaking grand staircase that curved down from the second floor. My footsteps echoed as I followed Stephen down the hall. He opened a set of glass French doors that led to a formal living room, then a formal dining room, and a kitchen big enough for a whole catering staff. All the while he talked, pointing out paintings, sculptures, and items of interest. He motioned towards a large bay window, through which I could see the pool and expansive gardens where all those parties I wasn't invited to took place.

"Do you want to see my room?" he asked sheepishly.

That was exactly what I came for, but I didn't want him to get the wrong idea. I wanted evidence, not a hook-up. Weighing my words, I said, "Sure . . . for a minute."

I followed him upstairs and down a long hallway. His room was huge, with a window overlooking the pool. Perry's pigsty, this was not. Stephen's bed was made, his computer desk clean, his dresser dust-free. It looked more like a hotel room than a teenage boy's room. The benefits of having a housekeeper, I guess.

I let my hand graze the surfaces as I roamed around the room. I made small talk so Stephen wouldn't suspect that I was psychically casing the joint.

"Your room is so nice," I said.

"My mother's neurotic about keeping everything orderly and organized. If I walk out of my room for a few minutes and leave a book on my desk, it's magically put away by the time I get back."

"That's not so bad," I said, my fingers lingering over his keyboard. "At least you don't have to clean it yourself."

He leaned against the wall, his feet crossed at his ankles. "Yeah, but I can't even have posters up."

"You can plaster your dorm room soon enough," I said, smiling, though on the inside I was anything but happy. This search was ending up a bust. I had glimmers of a few visions, but they were all irrelevant and mostly from the housekeeper cleaning. What I needed was a vision of that night at Yummy's.

Stephen babbled on about how much he was looking forward to college and getting out of Eastport. Meanwhile, I racked my brain. I needed something he had held on to that night in the restaurant. I tried to remember what he was wearing in the security video, but came up blank. I couldn't exactly ask him, either, without seeming suspicious. Then it hit me.

The only thing I remembered from the security tape was Cecile Clayworth's beautiful green dress. Cecile's wardrobe was so extensive, there was no way she'd worn that dress again in the past week. It might not have been sent to the cleaners, either.

"Is there a bathroom on this floor?" I asked, interrupting some story about his graduation party.

"Sure, down the hall on your right."

"OK. When I come back will you show me your pictures from graduation?"

Scrounging those up ought to keep him busy for a few minutes.

I scurried down the hall, guessing that the door at the end led to the master bedroom. I peeked in. Bingo. Now where was her closet? I pulled open a door and had to clap my hand over my mouth to prevent a gasp.

Cecile Clayworth's walk-in closet was like a dream. One entire wall of shelving held shoes. The other walls had racks of clothing . . . organized by colour.

It didn't take me long to find the emerald green dress I'd admired on the security tape. I let my fingers slip along the fabric as I opened my mind. Nothing surfaced at first, so I continued along the material until I reached the belt where Stephen's arm had been wrapped around his mother.

Then it came. Like a bullet.

I saw Stephen, obviously drunk, stagger up to where Victoria Happel sat on a bar stool. The noise level was deafening and I couldn't hear the words, but I figured he was hitting on her. Victoria rolled her eyes and put her hand up in his face, then turned away. Stephen's already ruddy cheeks turned bright red. He leaned closer and spoke in her ear, insistently.

The sights and sounds dimmed as feelings of anger boiled over and took control of the vision. Furious thoughts stirred in my mind.

She's going to ruin everything.

I've worked so hard to get to this point.

That little slut is not going to take it all away from me.

The emotions were so strong, I found myself gasping for air.

"What are you doing?"

I dropped the dress and whirled around. Stephen stood in the doorway of the closet, looking at me steadily.

"Nothing," I said, crossing my arms. "It's a beautiful dress."

"It's my mother's. What are you doing in her closet?"

I struggled to come up with something, anything that made the tiniest bit of sense. "She came to see me today," I blurted. "Told me to stay away from you. She said I wasn't good enough to date you. I didn't believe her."

I paused for dramatic effect. "But now I look at your big house with your mother's fancy walk-in closet. Any one of these dresses cost more than my whole wardrobe. And I'm thinking maybe she's right. I can't compete with the rich girls. I don't belong in this world."

Pass me the Academy Award. I don't know how I did it, but hysterical-girl tears sprung from my eyes as I ran out of the room and down the grand staircase.

He followed me. "Clare, wait!"

"I'm going to walk home!" I yelled.

"It's too far! Wait!"

But I was out of the door before he could catch up.

Rather than walk down the street, where he could easily find me, I darted into the woods. I called Justin from my mobile, hoping like hell he'd pick up, and he did.

"Clare?"

"Justin, I'm in trouble."

TWENTY-FOUR

In the woods, crackling twigs, incessant insect chirping, and other night noises were freaking me out. I huddled behind a tree in the darkness, alternating my eyes from the road to the brightly lit front door of the Clayworth house. Stephen had called out from the driveway, then shrugged and plodded back into the house. He hadn't come back out since.

How much of a stone-cold killer could he be if he didn't follow me out here? But the vision . . . the emotions in it were so strong. Stephen had been so angry at Victoria. Angry enough to kill.

But something about the vision nagged at me. My instinct was telling me I was off. I was missing something, seeing something wrong.

A black car slowed and pulled to the shoulder of the road. I moved a little closer, saw Justin on the driver's side, and ran for it.

Justin pulled a U-turn after I jumped in the passenger side. "Twice in two days I'm breaking the law for you," he said.

"I know. I'm sorry. I should have called someone with a licence, but I was scared and my first instinct..." I trailed off because I didn't want to finish that sentence out loud.

"I don't mind," he said. "I'll always come to your rescue. But I *would* like to know why I'm picking you up at night from the woods next to the Clayworth house."

"I had a sort-of date with Stephen tonight."

He clenched his jaw but remained silent.

"Not a real date," I continued. "I was using him."

"You've developed a habit for that," he muttered.

I ignored his comment and explained, "He was at Yummy's the night of Victoria's murder. He might have seen something that could help Perry."

"Like what?"

"I was hoping to find out if Gabriel interacted with Victoria when he was there."

"And?"

Justin ran a red light, but I was in no position to complain about his driving skills, so I continued. "Stephen said he didn't see anything. I got a vision, though, while I was in his house."

"What did you see?"

"Stephen talking to Victoria. I assume he was hitting on her. She rejected him. Then I felt strong humiliation and anger."

Justin pulled into my driveway. "Those are normal feelings when you get rejected by a girl."

"Not to this degree. I have never felt emotions so strong from a vision."

But Justin wasn't listening to me any more. He was glaring at something over my shoulder. I turned and looked out of the car window. Gabriel sat on the porch steps, elbows on his knees, obviously waiting for me.

"You two normally work together this late?" Justin asked.

"We're not working together at all any more."

I got out of the car and Gabriel rose, stuffing his hands in the pockets of his jeans. His black hair was a mess, as if he'd been pulling his fingers through it.

"Your mom said you were out," he began, walking towards me, "but I decided to wait for you. I'm sorry about the argument yesterday. I wanted to talk to you—"

He broke off as he saw Justin get out of the car.

"He's your date?" Gabriel asked.

"No," Justin said. "I'm the first one she called when the date went bad."

I think the correct term for this was "pissing contest", and though I was flattered, I didn't have time for it.

"Both of you," I said, hooking a thumb towards the house. "Inside. Now."

Mom was on the sofa, flipping through a magazine. "How was your dinner?" she asked, and then her mouth fell open as she watched both Justin and Gabriel come in behind me.

"Not one of my best," I said. "How was that last-minute reading?"

She groaned. "After all that begging on the phone, she never showed."

"Huh." I motioned to my two boys. "We have stuff to talk about. We're going upstairs."

Mom didn't exactly give me permission, but she knew I wasn't going to have an orgy in my room or anything. I led them to my bedroom and closed the door. I sat in my desk chair while the boys sat on the bed. They looked kind of silly, sitting there next to each other on top of my purple duvet. I suppressed a smile and filled Gabriel in on what I was doing out with Stephen Clayworth and the vision I had had in his house. Of course, I left out the part about my suspecting Gabriel prior to the vision. I still wondered about his tattoo, but was now convinced the murderer had to be Stephen and not Gabriel.

Gabriel's first instinct was the same as Justin's. "Who wouldn't feel bad after being rejected?"

"This was more than regular anger. It felt like..." I looked up at the ceiling while searching for the right words. "Imminent violence. Like his brain was snapping. He couldn't take any more."

I paused and shook my head.

"What?" Gabriel asked.

"Something about the vision doesn't make sense, but I can't put my finger on what it is. Something's nagging at me. I can almost catch it, but I just don't know."

"Maybe you have feelings that are clouding it," Justin said.

I considered that for a moment. "It's true that I can't picture Stephen killing anyone. Or maybe I just don't want it to be true."

"Plus," Justin said, "Stephen was plastered that night. You saw the tape. He could barely walk, much less point a gun straight."

That was true. This wasn't adding up. I dragged my hands through my hair in frustration.

"He should at least be taken in and questioned, though," Justin added.

Gabriel nodded. "I'll talk to my father in the morning."

"The morning?" Justin snapped. "Why not now?"

Gabriel gave an exaggerated sigh. "First of all, we don't have any evidence. Visions don't count for anything." He glanced at me. "And I've learned not to jump to conclusions about people's guilt."

"You're talking about Perry," I said. "You believe me now that he didn't do it?"

Gabriel nervously wiped his hands back and forth on his jeans. "There are things I should have told you before, to help explain why I initially acted the way I did towards you. But they're hard to talk about."

I waited for him to continue. Justin shifted uncomfortably.

"Years ago, my little sister was abducted," Gabriel began. "She's never been found. We assume she's dead."

I gasped. "I'm so sorry."

Gabriel leaned forward and pressed the palm of his hand on his forehead. I knew he was holding back intense emotions, trying to stay strong as he told the story.

"My father used every spare moment to work the streets. He staked out known paedophiles. Searched dumpsters. Questioned countless people." He paused. "My mother took a different route."

"What did she do?" Justin asked softly.

"She spent all our money on psychics and mediums, and then pressed my father to waste his time running down their fake leads."

Gabriel stood and began pacing back and forth. "One lady said my sister was dead, tossed in some pond. We paid divers to look and found nothing. One lady said she was sold into the sex trade in Thailand. My mom spent thousands of dollars flying over there and searching for her. It was obvious to Dad and I that these people were all frauds, using my mother's grief and desperation to make themselves a buck. But Mom kept going to more and more of these people, despite the fact that they all gave her different answers."

Gabriel's voice began to tremble. He took a moment to collect himself. "It eventually led to the destruction of their marriage. She's married to the bottle now."

"Is that why you moved here?" I asked. "Because of the divorce?"

"No, there's more. Another girl was kidnapped. She was the same age as my sister was when she disappeared. They tracked down her abductor to this abandoned building. The girl was already dead when my father got there. Dad tried to get information out of the perp about my sister. The guy resisted arrest, they fought, the gun went off. Long story short, he ended up dead. No one shed any tears for that man. But my father lost his job. The powers that be determined that he used excessive force. We moved here to start over. And we're still no closer to finding my sister. I'm starting to make peace with the fact that we never will."

We all stayed silent for a few moments. I was overwhelmed and had no idea what to say. I sat with my hand over my mouth as I replayed everything Gabriel had done and said with a new understanding. No wonder his father wanted no part of me helping the investigation. No wonder Gabriel had assumed I was a fraud from the start.

"What's your sister's name?" Justin asked.

"Victoria Toscano. We called her Vicki. She would be thirteen now."

I reeled back in my chair. Gabriel's tattoo wasn't proclaiming love for Victoria Happel. He had nothing to do with her. His tattoo was in remembrance of his sister. I wanted to punch myself in the face.

Gabriel's gaze locked on to me. "So, I'm sorry if I was a jerk."

"I can see why you'd have a thing against psychics," I offered. "But you know that I'm not defrauding the people who come to see me, right? I'd never lie to them."

"I admit that you're different, but I still don't believe in any of this. I hope that doesn't stop us from—" He glanced at Justin, then back at me. "Being friends."

"Of course not," I said.

"I should have told you sooner, but I can't bear to talk

about her. It's too painful. And my father wanted a fresh start. But after our fight I decided it might be helpful for you to see it from my point of view. That's why I came tonight."

I put my hand up to shush him. "Wait."

Gabriel spread his hands wide. "What did I say?"

"Point of view. That's it." I stood up, twisting my fingers around each other, my heart racing as the answer clicked into place.

Justin said, "Clare, what are you talking about?"

"That's what was bothering me. I *did* get the vision wrong. It wasn't Stephen's vision at all."

Gabriel and Justin looked at each other. "Huh?"

"My visions are always from the point of view of the person having the experience." I thought back to my vision of Victoria's murder. I didn't watch her get shot, I felt it.

Justin rose, quickly understanding. "So if you saw Stephen's face in the vision, it couldn't have been Stephen's experience. It was someone else watching it all unfold."

I nodded. "Someone else was feeling all that anger and hatred. Someone watching. Someone else who touched Cecile's belt."

Realization dawned on me like a thunderbolt. "It was Cecile," I said. "It all makes sense. It was her dress. We saw her on the tape. She walked in, left with Stephen, and then at some point came back. Cecile Clayworth killed Victoria Happel."

"That's an interesting theory," Gabriel said.

My head snapped towards him. "Why?"

"She was the one who called and placed Perry at the scene."

"*Cecile* was the mystery witness?" I was about to ask why Gabriel hadn't told me but realized that once Perry was taken into custody, he would naturally stop sharing case information with me.

"She said she saw Perry and the victim leaving Yummy's arm in arm," Gabriel said.

"Which is true," Justin noted. "She could have been doing her duty to help the investigation."

"Or to point it in the direction she wanted," I said.

"I don't buy her as the killer," Justin said. "Plus, going around shooting Billy and Joni to shut them up? She's too prim and proper for that."

"She's also a coldhearted bitch," I said. "Everyone knows that." I grabbed Gabriel's arm. "It's her. I know it. You have to tell your father to question her."

"We don't have any evidence," Gabriel said.

"What evidence did you have on my brother when you took him in and searched my house?"

"We had a witness place him with the victim the night of her murder."

"Well now I'm a witness who's placing Cecile Clayworth with the victim the night of the murder!"

"There's no motive!"

He was right. Though I was convinced Cecile had killed Victoria, I didn't know why. What had got her so angry? Watching her son get rejected would rile any mother, but not push them to the point of murder. I thought back to the vision again, the thoughts about Victoria ruining everything Cecile had worked for. This wasn't a random killing. There was history there. If only Cecile could be brought into the station and questioned, the police might be able to get the information out of her. Or she might even break down and confess.

"I heard her thoughts. Felt her emotions. I know it's her. Play fair, Gabriel," I said, desperately. "I know you think my visions are worthless. But give me this one chance to prove myself."

I didn't care if Justin was watching, I grabbed Gabriel's hands in mine and squeezed them. "Please."

"My father will never bring in a suspect or request a warrant based on a psychic vision," Gabriel said.

Justin stepped over to us. "Then lie."

"Excuse me?" Gabriel dropped my hands.

"If you care about Clare at all and I'm guessing you do, then lie." Justin's face was set in rigid determination. "Tell your father you found a witness who saw Cecile and Victoria get into it at the restaurant that night. There's no need to mention the vision."

Gabriel looked at me, and I pleaded with my eyes.

"Unless you don't trust Clare," Justin said. "If you think she's a liar and a fraud like the others you've run into. If you think that, do nothing. If you believe in her, like I do, then you'll do the right thing."

Gabriel stared at the rug. "I need to think about this."

"Please, Gabriel," I said.

"I'll call you." He turned and left.

I tossed and turned all night, dreaming of Cecile Clayworth chasing me through the woods, a knife held high, an evil smile on her face. I still didn't understand why Cecile would have gone on a killing spree. I felt like I had all the pieces, but I couldn't fit them together. Maybe I was trying to force one into the wrong place. But I knew in my heart Cecile had killed Victoria. The force of the emotions in my vision convinced me of that.

My mobile phone chirped on my nightstand. I reached for it, expecting it to be the middle of the night, but the clock said eight a.m.

"Gabriel?" I said, rubbing my eyes. He must have come to his decision. I hoped he'd made the right one and decided to trust me.

"No, it's Justin."

I sighed. Gabriel didn't believe me. He hadn't told his father. I'd have to find another way to prove Cecile's guilt and save my brother. I'd have to start all over.

"Good news," Justin said. "Detective Toscano just brought Cecile Clayworth into the station."

I bolted upright in bed. "Seriously?"

"I'm calling from my dad's office. He promised to come upstairs and fill me in on the details as they happen. I'll call you with updates."

"Screw that," I said. "I'll be there in a few."

I'd told Mom last night about my vision of Cecile and now ran into her room to tell her the good news. Mom was sitting up in bed, scratching her head. Her eyes widened at my harried entrance.

"What's got you all riled up?" she asked sleepily.

"They're questioning Cecile Clayworth at the station right now. Justin said we can go wait for updates with him in his father's office."

Mom bolted up from the bed and began pacing the room. "This could all be over," she said, pulling a sundress from a hanger in her closet and clutching it to her chest. She looked up at me with anxiously excited eyes.

"Should we wake Perry?" I asked.

"No, let him sleep. He hasn't had a good night's sleep in days. We'll give him the news later when he wakes up."

I gave her a few minutes to get dressed and ready, then handed her the keys to Perry's car, since hers was still minus one working tyre. The drive downtown was a blur, and before I knew it, we had arrived. The morning sunshine glinted off the windows of the town hall. I felt like things were falling into place. Everything was going to be all right. Mom must have read my thoughts because she grabbed my hand and smiled as we walked upstairs to the mayor's office.

Justin greeted us. "Morning, Clare. Morning, Mrs Fern."

My hesitant smile turned radiant as Justin gave me an encouraging nod. I felt light, almost like floating, at the prospect of my burdens lifting.

"Is your father downstairs in the station?" Mom asked.

"Yes. He's going to come up to give us an update when he can."

I heard quick footsteps on the stairs and turned to find Nate, out of breath.

"I knew I'd find you guys here," he said. "Where's Perry?"

"Sleeping," I said. "We'll wake him up when there's news. Hopefully she'll confess and this will all be over."

I took Nate by the arm out into the hallway, leaving my mother and Justin in the office.

"Listen," I said. "I don't think you should run the story about the Toscanos. It's not what you think."

"I know," Nate said.

I arched an eyebrow. "How?"

"I got in touch with the ex-Mrs Toscano. I finally caught her sober."

"So you know? About Gabriel's little sister?"

"Yeah. I'm letting it go."

I hugged him. "Thank you."

Loud footsteps came up the stairs, bringing my curious mother and Justin out into the hallway.

Mr Spellman reached the landing and his eyes widened. Apparently he wasn't expecting this much of a crowd outside his office.

"Is Cecile talking?" Mom asked.

"Not yet. She just made her one phone call," Mr Spellman said.

"To who?" I asked.

"Her lawyer, I'd assume."

"That's not good," Justin said, shaking his head.

Nate's phone beeped, and he flipped it open. "Interesting," he said, reading the text message.

"What is it?" I asked.

"My boss says the Clayworth family is big into guns. Dallas and Stephen have won father-son competitions and even Cecile is trained."

"Maybe that will encourage the police to search their house for the murder weapon," Mom said.

"I have to go," Nate said, closing his phone. "My boss wants me to search through the archives for mentions of Cecile and guns and maybe even a photo of Cecile with a gun from some competition." He smiled. "Interns get all the glamorous work."

As Nate trotted off, Mr Spellman turned back to us. "Nothing's going to happen for a while now. Cecile's not talking until her lawyer gets here and then who knows how long it will take for her statement."

Mom said, "I still want to stay anyway. Clare, why don't you go back, get some breakfast and give Perry the news when he wakes up."

"I'll walk with you," Justin offered, and we walked out together.

Only a week ago, I never thought I'd find myself walking beside Justin, in peace. But here we were, strolling along, enjoying the beautiful warmth of the morning sun.

We didn't talk much, and I didn't mind. It was a comfortable silence. I didn't want to slap him or yell at him. I didn't want to fight about Tiffany. I didn't even think about him with Tiffany, which was strange, considering that was all I had thought about every time I'd seen him the past three months. I'd never really stopped caring about him, and now I felt close to him again.

Gabriel had believed me after all, enough to get his father to bring Cecile in, anyway. Both Gabriel and Justin had come through for me and my family. A warm glow spread throughout my body and as I took a deep breath of fresh air, I was enveloped in a sense of calm.

When we reached my house, he walked me up the porch steps and turned to leave. Suddenly, I realized I didn't want him to go.

"Want to come in for a drink or something?" I asked.

"Sure," he said with a wide smile.

I turned the knob, and the door opened. "Perry must be awake." I'd locked the door behind me when we left.

"Perry!" I called out.

No response.

Justin shrugged and said, "Must be in the shower."

I turned left to enter the kitchen, planning to grab us some Cokes from the fridge, then stopped short.

A body was on the floor.

All I saw were two feet sticking out from the other side of the kitchen island.

"Perry?" I squeaked.

I wanted to rush to his side, but a deep voice echoed in the foyer behind me.

"Don't. Move."

I slowly turned around and found a gun pointed at my head. My breath caught in my throat. I managed to squeeze out one word.

"You?"

TWENTY-FIVE

"Stand next to her," Stephen Clayworth yelled at Justin, waving the gun around. "Don't make any stupid moves."

I stood in shock, unable to move even if I'd wanted to.

Justin put his hands up and inched closer to me.

"Cecile didn't call the lawyer," Justin said. "She called you."

Stephen smiled. "Smart boy. You could be mayor someday."

"Stephen, what are you doing?" I asked. I couldn't believe this was happening. I was sure Cecile was the killer. The vision had been from her point of view.

"My mother called me with an order for one more mess to be cleaned up. But don't worry, I called the lawyer for her on my way over. She'll be fine. You all, however." He grinned, and his face transformed. It was a Stephen I'd never seen before.

"Perry is unconscious in the kitchen," he continued. "His prints will be all over this weapon. My mother and I will be free. And you will be dead and out of our hair for ever."

Stephen pointed the gun at me.

Justin let out a roar and charged towards him. Stephen aimed, fired off a shot, and Justin stopped like he'd hit a brick wall. He fell backwards, and his body slammed on to the floor.

"No!" I screamed and fell to my knees beside Justin. Blood seeped from his body, too much, too fast. The room spun, and I squinted and tried to focus. I stared at Justin's chest, but couldn't see the telltale rise and fall of breathing.

"Sorry about your loverboy," Stephen said. "But you won't have long to mourn him. You're next."

I stood up to face him and he slammed the gun against my head. I fell back down to the floor in a dizzy slump. Sticky blood dripped down my forehead. Why did he do that? Why not just shoot me?

I looked up at him as realization dawned. "You want me unconscious."

He narrowed his eyes at me. "What?"

"You can't kill me when I'm awake and looking at you. You can't."

"Don't tell me what I can't do. I've already killed two people."

I gave him a blank look. "Two?"

"Mother made a mistake by killing that bitch. We could have dealt with her in other ways. I tried. But Mother had reached the end of her rope."

"So your mother did kill Victoria," I said, wincing as my head started to throb. "Why?"

"Because she was a little slut who wouldn't take no for an answer," he spat.

I shook my head in confusion. "Was she your girlfriend or something?"

"No! She was one of my father's . . . dalliances. He only saw her a few times, when he'd go to Boston. He thought he was perfectly clear about their situation. But something set that little bimbo off and she thought she could come down here." He started laughing now, almost maniacally. "That idiot actually thought she could be more than a mistress."

Voices echoed in my head. Nate had said the paper was investigating a possible Dallas Clayworth mistress. Joni had mentioned that she and Victoria cater-waitered fancy parties in Boston. Joni also pointed out that it was out of character for Victoria to come down here without knowing anyone and that in those final weeks, she'd been keeping a secret.

I did have all the pieces. I just hadn't put them together.

Victoria met Dallas at one of his fundraisers and they'd started an affair. She was fine keeping it quiet until her life at home fell apart. She lost her boyfriend and her best friend. So she decided to come down here to try to take her thing with Dallas to the next level.

"Dallas turned her away," I said, lifting my eyes to Stephen's.

"And then she tried to force his hand." Stephen's nostrils flared. "She threatened to go public. He'd lose the election."

"Still," I said. "She didn't have to die."

"My mother tried to reason with her on the phone," Stephen said.

I remembered my vision, when I'd touched Victoria's mobile.

You don't own him. He doesn't want you any more. He wants me.

I'd assumed Victoria had been fighting with Joni over Joel. But no. She'd been fighting with Cecile. Over her husband.

Stephen stared at a spot over my shoulder as if remembering a moment. "I even tried to reason with her myself, that night. I told her to leave my family alone and go back to Boston."

I remembered Stephen in the vision, whispering insistently in Victoria's ear.

He brought his eyes back to my face. "But none of it worked. So Mother decided to take things into her own hands. To protect our family and our future. She sent me home in a cab and then followed the girl and your brother back to the motel. She waited for Perry to leave, then went in and shot her with this gun. My father has a sizable collection. If the police search my house, they won't even realize one is missing."

"She told you she was going to do this?" I asked, hoping to keep him talking.

"No. But then that idiot Billy Rawlinson tried to blackmail her and she needed help. She told me to meet him and clean up that mess."

"And Joni?"

"I did what had to be done."

"Why?"

"That twit started her own investigation. She went to Yummy's asking around about what guys Victoria had talked to that night. My mother saw her putting posters up. She got too close. So I had to take care of that, too. Both of them would be alive now if they'd minded their own business."

Pain radiated up from my knees, but I was too scared to adjust my position on the floor. I didn't want to move one inch. I just wanted to keep him talking because, so far, that was the only thing keeping me alive. "So you're saying they deserved it," I said.

"I had to kill both of them, don't you see? To protect my family. And now I have to kill you to protect my family. But you're the last one. Your brother is in la-la land, ready to put his fingerprints on this gun – the murder weapon. He'll be put away for life for killing his sister and the mayor's son. There will be no doubt left about who killed the others, since he was already the main suspect anyway. I can go to college, get away and start over."

He swallowed hard. "I'm sorry about this, Clare. Truth be told, I liked you. I really did. That's why I didn't kill you right away after I saw you with Billy's body, trying to use your ability."

I felt paralysed. Every muscle in my body was stretched tight. "That was you in the woods watching me."

"I gave you a second chance to come to your senses and mind your own business. But you didn't. You kept pushing. Now I have no choice. My mother never should have started this. But I have to finish it."

Maslov had been right. Stephen said she'd told him a redhead would bring him trouble, and I had. And she told me I was in mortal danger, and I was.

My breath came in short gasps and my lungs ached. I blinked away a drop of blood that slid down my forehead. This was it. My last chance to reason with him. To beg for my life.

"You don't want to kill me," I said.

"Of course I don't, Clare. But I have to."

"This isn't you. You're not a murderer," I pleaded.

"A couple weeks ago, I would've said the same thing. But you should know more than anyone how people surprise you. People can do things you never imagined they would. You think you know someone and then. . ."

He shrugged and cocked the gun.

Then my world went black. A heavy weight landed on top of me. I was on my stomach, my face mashed into the floor. I heard a gunshot. Wood splintering. Stephen screaming. The sounds of struggle surrounded me. I couldn't see and needed to know what was happening. I pushed up on my hands and rolled the weight off my back. It made an *oomph* sound.

"Perry?"

His head was bleeding and his eyes were eerily dilated. Definitely a concussion, but Perry had come to enough to save me when it counted. The front door was open. Detective Toscano and another officer had Stephen down on the floor, forcing his hands into cuffs as he screamed and writhed like an animal.

Perry leaned over Justin's unmoving body and placed two fingers on his pulse.

Then he looked at me.

TWENTY-SIX

"I really think you should go home," Mom said. "Get some rest."

My fingers gingerly touched the bandage on my forehead. "I'm resting here."

"Me too," Perry said from the chair beside me. He had a matching bandage on his head. We looked like two idiots who'd decided to have a headbutting competition.

We'd been at the hospital for hours. My injury wasn't bad. All it needed was some Tylenol and gauze. Perry had to have three stitches and he had a minor concussion, but he'd be fine.

Justin . . . we didn't know yet.

Gabriel returned to the waiting area with an armful of cold bottled waters, which we all grabbed and gulped.

"Gabriel," my mother said, leaning forward in her chair.

"How did your father know that my children were in trouble?"

Gabriel took a long swig of water. "This crazy lady called the station, freaking out, screaming that we had to go to your house right now."

"Huh," Mom said, pulling back her frazzled hair into a low ponytail. "Milly must have heard the commotion."

Gabriel shrugged. "Whoever she was, she had a strong Russian accent. That's all I know."

Madame Maslov. I shivered. She must have had a vision of the confrontation and called the police just in time. I swallowed hard. I'd prejudged her just like so many people prejudged me. And I was wrong. She was no more a fraud than I was.

I went around the corner to toss my empty bottle in the recycling bin. Gabriel followed me. When we were alone, he gathered me to him and held me close, resting his chin on the top of my head. I sank into his embrace, sharing the weight of my emotions and exhaustion on his shoulders.

"I'm sorry," he said, his voice soft. "You were right about the Clayworths."

"Half right," I said, sadly, pulling away. If I'd got the whole picture, I could have saved Justin.

"Half is more than I gave you credit for."

"But you trusted me in the end. Enough to tell your father to bring Cecile in."

"I also want to apologize for suspecting your brother."

I forgave him quickly for that one, because I'd made a lot of quick and wrong assumptions lately, too.

"I want to know something," Gabriel said. He took a deep breath. "Could we start over? Is there any way you could give me another chance?"

Before I could even think about Gabriel's question, I saw movement over his shoulder. Mr Spellman was speed walking down the hallway. I sprinted over to him as he reached the waiting area. Mom and Perry stood up.

"How is he?" Mom asked.

"The surgery was successful and he's awake. We've been talking and everything. He's going to be fine."

My heart soared. I let out a deep breath I felt like I'd been holding in for hours.

A collective relieved murmur went around the room.

"My wife will only agree to go to the cafeteria if someone else keeps him company." Mr Spellman looked at me and I nodded quickly.

I dashed down the hallway and hurtled myself into the room, careful not to let the door slam behind me. Justin lay on the bed, eyes closed, face grey. His shirt was off and a large white bandage covered the left side of his abdomen.

I closed my eyes and inhaled deeply through my nose. The relief was overwhelming. It was almost as if I couldn't believe that he was all right until I saw it myself.

"Clare," Justin said.

I rushed over to the side of the bed. "You're awake."

"Yeah, I was just resting my eyes. I'm so happy to see you. I'm so glad you're OK."

"How are you feeling?"

Justin inched up a bit on the bed and winced. "Being shot sucks. I'll be honest. But it was worth it if it saved you." He smiled weakly.

"I don't know what I'd do if I lost you," I said.

"You're just saying that because I nearly died saving your ass."

I laughed. "I'm not. I realized it when I kissed you on the boardwalk."

His eyebrows lifted.

"But that doesn't mean I want to get back together."

"We will," he said, crossing his arms on his lap. "It's just a matter of time now."

"You're very confident."

"Maybe I can see the future." He winked.

"Is there room for two more in this lovefest?" Perry asked, poking his head into the room.

"Absolutely, dude," Justin said.

Perry and Gabriel sauntered in.

"Dude," Justin said, laughing at Perry. "Nice headband."

"It must be on too tight." Perry reached up and fingered the bandage. "I have quite the headache."

"I've got to thank your dad, man," Justin said to Gabriel, shaking his hand. "The doctor said if I'd been lying there much longer, I would have bled to death."

I watched the small talk continue between Gabriel and Justin. My eyes darted from one to the other and I felt so conflicted. I decided it was time to go. Too many butterflies for me in this room.

I backed out into the hallway, careful not to trip over a gurney someone had left beside the door.

"Clarity."

I turned and found Madame Maslov hurrying down the hall towards me. "Your mother said I could find you here. I had things to say to her and I need to say them to you as well."

"You were the one," I said.

She stopped short. "What is it you speak of now?"

"You slashed my mom's tyre before we were about to go to the Clayworth house the first time. Then you called in with a fake appointment before I left the next time. Why didn't you just tell me I was in danger?"

She put her hands on her hips and gave me a look.

"Oh yeah." I smirked, remembering. "You did tell me."

"As I said before, you're not good with the listening."

"But you didn't give me any specifics."

"I did not know the who or the why. I just felt when you were about to be in trouble. I did what I could."

"Thank you for that." I grabbed her hand. "I'm sorry my family hasn't exactly been welcoming to you. That will change now."

"Now?" She cackled. "Just as I am leaving?"

"You're leaving town? Why?"

"The purpose I was brought here for, was not nice." She did a tsk-tsk motion with her finger.

"What do you mean?"

"I was ... what is the word in English? Recruited. Someone paid for my rent, paid for my advertising and all I had to do was my readings and please my customers. I thought this was a great deal. What a wonderful country, this America, with these investors. But now I have realized that I was part of plan to make revenge on your family. I do not agree with this."

It all made sense now. Why Stephen was in Maslov's shop that day on the boardwalk. Why I saw Cecile walking towards it before our argument. "It was Cecile Clayworth who paid you."

"Yes," she answered.

It was payback for my snitching on Stephen in school. Damn, vengeance was like a hobby to that family.

"I am sorry for this trouble I have helped with." Maslov patted me on the cheek and turned to go.

"Wait," I said. "Before you go . . . can I have tomorrow's lottery numbers?"

She threw her head back and laughed. "No. No numbers of the lottery. But I will leave you with a quick reading."

She sidled up next to me, as if sharing a secret, and clasped my hand tightly between hers. She made a clucking sound and shook her head slowly. "I see two things in your future. One soon and one later. Soon, your brother will injure his ankle. And, later . . . someone's love for you is not genuine . . . their feelings are not born of affection, but of sickness. . ." Her eyes snapped open and she dropped my hand. "Be wary."

"OK . . . thanks." I gave an involuntary shiver. Maslov had known when I was in danger before, sure, but this didn't mean anything. Right? She was probably fifty-fifty, hit or miss. I hoped.

"One more question." I looked both ways down the hallway to make sure my mother wasn't hanging around. "The man you saw who looked like my brother. Was he old enough to be my father?"

Maslov's eyes narrowed. "Why do you ask this?"

"I haven't seen or heard from my father in fifteen years."

She frowned, her lips pressed tightly together. "He could be. The comparison in looks was uncanny. But..."

"But what?"

"If he is your father, be glad he's not here."

Before I had a chance to digest that nugget, the door to Justin's room opened behind me. I glanced over my shoulder and saw Perry saying his goodbyes to Justin. When I looked back, Maslov was already halfway down the hall.

"Crap," I said.

"Whoa! Whoa!"

I whirled around in time to watch Perry trip over the gurney, twist sideways, and land on the floor. He yelped like a little girl.

While holding his ankle.

Later, when Mom finally allowed me to be out of her sight for a minute, I strolled down to the beach and sat on the warm sand. I scooped up a handful and let the grains slip through my fingers and drift away on the wind. Foam-tipped waves rushed forth and back, to the delight of squealing children, running with their pails, not a care in the world.

I thought about Justin and Gabriel and my confusing feelings for both of them.

I thought about Maslov's grim words about the man who could be my father and her dire warning about someone's intentions towards me.

And finally, I thought about Stephen and what he had done. In a twisted way, I could understand his motives. I knew about loyalty, about putting family before all others. I'd already learned some things I'd do to protect my own. I'd withhold information from the police. I'd use people. I'd lie.

If pushed harder . . . how far would I go? Stephen had found that out.

Hopefully I'd never have to know my own limits.

ACKNOWLEDGEMENTS

My heartfelt thanks to:

Scott Miller, my agent, for taking a chance on me.

The entire Scholastic team. You are all made of awesome. Especially Aimee Friedman, editor extraordinaire. You had me at *Veronica Mars*.

Susan Happel Edwards, for the title. And for being a hilarious, thoughtful, generous, smart, and fantastic friend. And a Hooplehead.

Ted Curtin, for security camera info. Maybe in a future novel I'll use something more high tech!

The creators of the Xbox 360, for keeping my husband and son busy while I write.

The Poker Crew, for Friday night laughs.

The LOC girls, for many years of friendship.

All the teen and adult readers, bloggers, booksellers,

and librarians who have shown early enthusiasm for the book . . . thank you, thank you, thank you!

Many other friends, old and new, too many to name, who I adore and appreciate. Thanks for your support and for all the good times.

My parents, Dan and Barbara Harrington; my "outlaws", Ann and Tony; and my entire extended family – all of you crazy people – from Massachusetts to Ireland. I love you!

Mike and Ryan, who make me smile, laugh, and feel loved every day. I'm the luckiest chick on the planet. Except for that lady who won the lottery five times. But I still wouldn't trade places with her.

If you liked CLARITY
look out for more
by Kim Harrington. . .

Turn over for an exclusive look
at the sequel to CLARITY

PERCEPTION

Coming March 2013

ONE

I stepped forward with forced confidence. "Let's do this."

I reached out and took the knife, the wooden handle heavy in my hand. For a moment, it felt like everything in me froze. As if even my blood stopped rushing through my veins.

I thought about the events of the last few days and wished I could have pieced things together sooner. Maybe then, I wouldn't be standing here with a knife and a girl's life in my hands. Every muscle in my body tightened in preparation for what I was about to do.

For what I had to do.

I raised the knife above my shoulder. She looked up at me with widened eyes and trembling lips. And with all my strength, I plunged the knife down.

TWO
SIXTEEN DAYS EARLIER

I jumped when my bagel popped up from the toaster.

"A bit on edge this morning, are we?" Mom said, buttering her toast.

"Nah. It's quiet in here, and that toaster shoots these things out at warp speed." I plucked the bagel out with my fingertips. "Ouch, ouch, ouch."

"It's hot," Mom said.

"Wow, you are psychic!" I joked.

She gently patted me on the face as she brought her plate to the kitchen table. Mom wore a mauve Indian print dress that hung down to her bare feet. Her mass of red curls was tied up in a loose bun. Looking at her was kind of like looking into the future. My mom and I share the same red hair, freckles, blue eyes, and petite frame. Though I definitely won't dress like her when I'm in my forties, unless I fall victim to some midlife personality disorder.

She glanced up from her plate. "Joining me or taking your bagel on the go?"

"I'll join," I said. "I've got some time before school."

"Good, bring the OJ."

I grabbed the jug from the fridge and settled into a wooden chair at the table. "Perry still sleeping?"

Mom grunted in reply.

"Any appointments today?" I asked, quickly changing the subject.

Mom shook her head sadly. I wasn't surprised. It was the end of September and the tourists were gone.

My brother, mother, and I live in a purple Victorian house on the main drag in Eastport, Massachusetts, on Cape Cod. Our family business is in . . . well, entertainment, I guess. The sign outside our home advertises: Readings by the Fern Family. My mother, Starla, is a telepath. She can read minds. My brother, Periwinkle "Perry" Fern, is a medium who can contact the dead.

And me? My full name is Clarity Fern, but I go by Clare. I have a gift called retrocognitive psychometry. I can't predict the future, but I can see the secrets in the past. When I touch an object and concentrate, I can sometimes see visions or feel emotions from when someone else touched the same thing.

Readings can be one-on-one or all three of us working together. Most of our business comes from tourists during the summer months, and we have to budget that money to last throughout the year.

Most townies love it when September comes and the tourists leave for the season. The traffic clears up. The beaches empty. Things slow down. But I've always found it sort of sad. Watching the seasonal businesses close down. The empty lifeguard towers on the beach. Vacancy signs on every motel. The gray skies that foretold of a long winter to come. Knowing I had months of school and therefore torture ahead of me.

Although things were different this year.

My phone buzzed in the pocket of my jeans, and I slid it out and took a peek. A text from Gabriel Toscano.

Want a ride?

I couldn't help the smile that overtook my face. I typed back.

Sure

"Is it Gabriel?" Mom asked, and I nodded, still grinning.

"Are you dating him?" she pressed on, and I didn't answer.

Steam rose from her teacup, trailed up into the air, and disappeared. Her eyebrows went up and I knew what she was about to do. The thing that made me so angry, I imagined fireworks shooting out of my ears.

She was going to read my mind.

So I focused all my energy on a message and silently repeated it over and over.

Stop invading my privacy, you peeping Mom!

She cocked her head to the side and sighed. "No need to call me names, Clarity."

Almost all mothers are busybodies, always wanting to know every detail of their daughters' lives. I get that. And I was glad Mom wasn't one of those distant, unloving mothers who didn't care enough to bug her kids with questions. But being a telepath gave my mom an unfair advantage and I hated when she used it. If she wanted to know about my love life, she should do what other mothers do: politely ask questions that remain unanswered until the daughter decides to toss her mother a bone over a shared pint of ice cream.

I gulped the last of my OJ as another text came from Gabriel.

Outside now

I pulled back the white lace curtain and peeked out the window. Sure enough, Gabriel's red Jeep was out there idling. He'd already been almost here when he texted me. He knew I'd say yes.

I yelled a "bye" to Mom, slung my black book bag over my shoulder, and darted down the porch steps. I gave a quick wave to Milly, our neighbor, who was crossing the front yard. She often came over to share town gossip with Mom.

I slowed my walk on the driveway, not wanting to appear too excited. Though it was a bright and sunny morning, the fall air was crisp and stung my cheeks. I zipped my gray hoodie, then hitched my jeans up a bit when I realized a slice of stomach was showing.

Not fast enough, apparently. Gabriel's eyes lingered on my midsection a beat too long, then snapped up to my face.

If he were Justin Spellman, my ex-boyfriend turned friend, I'd toss out a snarky remark about staring. But Gabriel and I weren't on those comfortable terms yet. We were still feeling each other out, learning what made each other tick. And Gabriel was a hothead. I never knew when he'd take a comment the wrong way.

Plus, I didn't exactly mind that he was staring.

I climbed into the passenger seat and dropped my bag on the floor. Gabriel fiddled with the radio and I snuck a peek at him. He wore baggy jeans and a white T-shirt that contrasted well against his tanned arms. His black hair was a bit longer than the short cut he'd had over the summer, a little windblown with the hint of a curl against his neck.

He stretched his arm over the back of my headrest and leaned toward me. For a moment, I thought he was going in for a kiss, but then I realized he'd put the car into reverse and was just angling to see out the rear window as we backed into the street.

I let out a breath I'd been holding in. Had I wanted him to kiss me again? I didn't know, so I forced the thought out of my mind.

Gabriel and I had met over the summer under intense circumstances. He had just moved to town and was the son of our new detective. When I got involved in the case of a tourist's murder, I was partnered with Gabriel. Much to his dismay.

Years ago, Gabriel's little sister was kidnapped. She'd never been found. His mother had spent all the family's money on psychics. One psychic would say her body was in such-and-such a lake. They'd dredge the lake, nothing. The other would say she was in Bangkok; they'd fly to Bangkok, nothing. But his mother kept believing whatever the psychics said, and kept wasting the family's time and money on these wild goose chases. It eventually caused Gabriel's parents' marriage to fail. His mother was constantly drunk now. He and his father moved to Eastport from New York to get some space.

So, naturally, Gabriel had a bit of an issue with psychics.

We had undeniable heat and shared a couple of swoon-worthy kisses over the course of the investigation. But we totally got off on the wrong foot, and I also had an unresolved situation with my ex-boyfriend who didn't want to remain ex.

So Gabriel and I were starting over. Trying to move past our differences and be friends.

Super-complicated friends.

"To what do I owe this honor?" I asked.

"Honor?" he repeated, turning forward and shifting the car into drive.

"Mr. Big Time hot new senior picking up little ol' me for a ride to school?"

The side of his mouth lifted in a half smile. "You think I'm hot?"

"The girls at school do. They even have a nickname for you."

"If it's those vapid blondes who follow you around everywhere, I don't even want to know what it is."

A year ago, the idea of anyone following me around would have made me howl with laughter. I was used to attention, but only the negative kind. Being a psychic in a family of paranormal freaks attracts that.

But when I started my junior year of high school a month ago, everything changed. Rather than tell me to get lost as I approached a cafeteria table, people actually asked me to sit next to them. When I walked by, people said, “Hi, Clare,” instead of snickering and calling me names.

It was all because of what went down over the summer. My showdown with a murderer, during which I nearly got killed myself, was the talk of the town. It was like I was a celebrity. But I didn’t ask for this newfound popularity and I didn’t really want it. It wasn’t me they liked. It was the story. Everyone wanted all the dirty details. How did I feel when the gun was pointed at my head? What was it like when Justin got shot? How did we get the bloodstain out of our hardwood floor?

Believe me, no question was out of bounds to those vultures.

“Okay, I won’t repeat the sentiments of any vapid blondes,” I replied, laughing. The good thing about Gabriel was you never had to wonder how he felt about anything. He made his opinions painfully clear. Even when I wished he’d keep them to himself. Not because he was wrong. Sometimes I didn’t want to listen to him because he was right.

“So who was that old lady going up to your house?” Gabriel asked as we drove down the street. “Is she like . . . a regular customer?”

“No, that was Milly. Our neighbor,” I said curtly. I

wasn't in the mood for Gabriel's high horse about psychics. He'd finally agreed that, maybe, my family and I weren't frauds looking to bilk grieving people out of their savings. But I knew he still didn't completely approve. One time he'd said that our seeing regular customers was feeding an addiction, like we were drug dealers or casino owners.

I was not going to take the bait this time. I gazed out the window at the passing stores and houses.

"What's wrong?" he prodded.

"I don't want to fight with you," I said, crossing my arms.

"Disagreeing and having a bit of back-and-forth is not fighting."

"Bickering, then," I said.

"For it to be bickering, we have to be annoyed with each other." His eyes left the road and instead traveled the length of my body. "And I'm anything but annoyed by you right now."

That was Gabriel's MO. Get me all pissed off, then say something flattering as if that would make it all better.

It usually did.

He parked the Jeep in the school lot and we both got out, causing a few second glances and raised eyebrows as we walked toward the school.

Gabriel leaned closer to me and whispered, "People are staring."

"They shouldn't be," I said, tossing a stern look at a group of sophomore girls. "Everyone knows we're friends."

"Maybe it looks like more than that to them."

"I don't get why it's so interesting. People need to stop theorizing and gossiping about others and focus on themselves," I said with a raised voice.

We'd reached the main doors, but Gabriel stopped walking. I turned to find him staring at me. I'd seen that intense gaze before, but it still started a fire inside me, beginning at my cheeks and spreading everywhere else.

In a low voice, he said, "Everyone in school assumes you and Justin are going to get back together."

I swallowed hard. "And what do you think?"

He stepped up to me and tucked a windblown curl behind my ear. "I think people shouldn't make assumptions." Then he turned and walked into the school.

Just then, Kendra Kiger and Brooke Addison — the so-called vapid blondes — marched up to me. It was good timing since I wasn't sure my legs could move yet and I didn't want to be standing there outside all alone and frozen in place like an idiot.

"What was he saying to you?" Kendra asked

breathlessly.

"He is so hot," Brooke said.

"Did he really drive you to school this morning?" Kendra asked.

I nodded. "We're friends."

"So hot," Brooke repeated, staring off into space.

Kendra rolled her eyes at Brooke. "But why did he drive you to school today?"

"He offered," I said.

They expected me to jump up and down and squee and giggle about how smokin' Gabriel was, but that's just not me.

I walked into the entrance hallway, which was painted a lovely shade of nursing-home gray. Kendra and Brooke followed closely at my side. I still wasn't used to their company. Kendra, Brooke, and their other friend, Tiffany Desposito, were the most popular girls in my class. All three were blond and pretty, but only Brooke was naturally so. Kendra had to try a bit harder, to overcome the hard angles of her face. Kendra was popular because she had money. Daddy bought her a nice car, and Mommy looked the other way when she wanted to throw parties in the McMansion. Meanwhile, Tiffany rose to the top by being so mean that everyone else was afraid to slight her.

Last year, the only interaction they'd had with me was

their daily attempt at verbal torture. But this year, Kendra and Brooke had gotten obsessed with my "magic powers" and desperately wanted me in their clique. I had no interest whatsoever, but I had to admit not being constantly bullied was a nice change of pace.

"Anyway, forget boy talk — we have some news," Brooke said, snapping me out of my thoughts.

It was then that I noticed the buzz surrounding us. Clumps of kids dotted the hallway, leaning in close, whispering and reacting in shocked tones. Something was going on.

"What news?" I asked.

Kendra put on her serious face. "Sierra Waldman is missing."

THREE

"Who?" I asked.

Brooke giggled. "That was my response, too. I don't think anyone knew her."

Kendra added, "She's a senior. New this year. I think she'd been homeschooled or something her whole life." She clucked her tongue. "Only here a month and now she's taken off. Some kids just can't handle public school."

I ignored Kendra's ignorant snap judgment. "How long has she been gone?"

"Apparently a few days, but word only got around today when her mom showed up in the school parking lot, yelling at kids." Kendra's eyes gleamed at the drama of it.

"What was she yelling about?"

Brooke twirled a long strand of blond hair around her finger. "Just asking everyone if they've seen her and all that."

"Does anyone know anything?" I asked, my interest piqued.

"There are a million rumors," Brooke said. "I heard she met a guy online and they ran away together."

"That doesn't make any sense," Kendra snapped. "She'd tell her mom."

"Maybe she knew her mom wouldn't let her go," Brooke said. "Maybe she would have disapproved of her guy. So she left without telling her."

I watched the conversation bounce back and forth like a Ping-Pong game until the homeroom bell rang. I followed the crowd, breaking off to file into our classrooms.

I felt sorry for the teachers who had to repeatedly try to regain control of their morning classes. Especially Mr. Rylander and Mr. Frederick — redirecting attention from juicy gossip to physics and algebra II were almost impossible feats. Sierra's disappearance was all people talked about through the morning and well into lunch. Rumors were spreading like a virus, but no one seemed to have any facts.

I ate my lunch in relative peace, listening to Kendra, Brooke, and the rest of the junior girls around me talking about Sierra. I realized that — for the first time this fall — the spotlight was not on me. And I liked it. Then I felt guilty because it came at the expense of someone else's problems.

I can't win.

But I also felt something else. A stirring inside. Something I hadn't felt since I was brought on board to help the police over the summer. I began to wonder if there was anything I could do to help find Sierra. Then I brushed the thought off. Sierra probably just had a fight with her mother, ran off, and would be back tomorrow.

When lunch ended, I dumped my tray and joined the crowd merging into the hallway, which was plastered with posters about the homecoming dance. I only had five minutes to get to my locker, grab my books, and make it to my next class. The herd was moving a little slow for me to accomplish all of that in time, so I zigged and zagged, apologizing when I accidentally hip-checked a freshman, and finally got to my locker. I spun the dial and started knocking off the numbers.

"They really should give us more time between periods," the girl at the locker beside mine said.

She wore a black T-shirt and a black skirt with fishnets. Her hair was also dyed black, with one bright blue streak on the side that fell in front of her face as she bent down to pick up a dropped notebook. I figured she was new in school. I would have definitely remembered her from last year. There aren't many people at Eastport High who stand out. Standing out is bad. I know this from experience.

"Seriously," I agreed. "It's like they want us to be late. I'm calling it detention entrapment."

She laughed heartily.

"Was it this bad at your old school?" I asked, figuring I'd be nice and reach out.

She straightened. "What do you mean?"

"You're new here, right?"

Her brow furrowed. "No, Clare Fern, I'm not." And with that, she turned on her heel and sped down the hallway.

"Clare, what did you say to her?" Kendra asked, appearing beside me.

"I asked if she was new in school," I said, still confused.

Kendra burst out laughing. "That's Mallory Neely."

Mallory Neely. I knew her, of course. She was the quiet girl, no friends that I knew of. She kept to herself, eyes cast down at all times, and never spoke unless spoken to. She was invisible. I'd actually felt slightly jealous of her in the past because I'd rather have been invisible like her than a big neon flashing bully target.

"I didn't realize it was her," I said.

"Why would you?" Kendra rolled her eyes. "No one notices Mallory. Except this year she shows up looking like a mall goth. Finally wanting some attention, I suppose."

I shrugged. "I think she looks cool."

Kendra bit her lip. This time last year, she'd have called me a freak, and now she wasn't even disagreeing with me. I felt like I'd entered a parallel universe.

"Hey," Kendra whispered, leaning in close to me. "You know the algebra quiz Mr. Frederick is planning?"

"Yeah . . ." I answered warily.

"Why don't you spend a few minutes in his classroom while he's in the teachers' lounge. And . . . you know . . ." She waggled her eyebrows. "See if you can use your powers to get us the answers."

I sighed, not bothering to hide my irritation. "No," I said simply. There were about ten thousand different reasons why I would do no such thing — fear of getting caught being one of them. But Kendra should have known by now I wasn't going to "Dance, Monkey, Dance!" whenever she asked. I wasn't some sideshow at a carnival. She had asked a couple times for me to do a reading of this or that at school. I always refused. If she truly wanted a reading, she could come to my place of business and pay like everyone else.

"What's up, Kendra," Tiffany said as she approached her locker, almost directly across the hall from mine. She sneered at me and said, "Hey, freak."

Apparently, Tiffany never got the "Clare's cool now" memo. No matter how much her friends supposedly liked me, she never would. Tiffany had always been the one to rally the anti-Clare troops and instigate all devious plans against me. She'd ramped up the torture last year after my brother, Perry, hooked up with her and never called her again. I had to suffer for my brother's man-whore ways. As part of her revenge plot, Tiffany had set her sights on my boyfriend at a party, and Justin had been dumb enough to fall for it. Yeah, alcohol was involved, but that's no excuse. It would take a lot more than tequila to make me lose my virginity to Satan.

"Don't mind her," Kendra whispered into my ear. Then she bolted over to Tiffany, probably to relay the "hilarious" story about how lame Mallory was.

I shook my head and focused on finding my history book. The bell was going to ring any second. I pulled the textbook out and a paper fluttered to the ground. I reached down, expecting to find an old quiz of mine, but it was a note. Written in all caps were three words:

YOU AMAZE ME.

I smiled and my stomach did that little butterfly thing.

And that was when Tiffany screamed.